ON
TRÀIGH LAR
BEACH

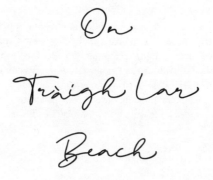

On Tràigh Lar Beach

A SHORT STORY COLLECTION

by

DIANNE EBERTT BEEAFF

SHE WRITES PRESS

Published 2020
Printed in the United States of America
ISBN: 978-1-63152-771-5 pbk
ISBN: 978-1-63152-772-2 ebk
Library of Congress Control Number: 2020907327

For information, address:
She Writes Press
1569 Solano Ave #546
Berkeley, CA 94707

She Writes Press is a division of SparkPoint Studio, LLC.

Book design by Stacey Aaronson

Original graphite drawings by Dianne Ebertt Beeaff were adapted from illustrations in the book *Scottish Wildflowers* and are printed by permission of HarperCollins Publishers, Ltd. (Michael Scott, 2012, taken from *New Generation Guide to the Wild Flowers of Britain and Northern Europe*, Alastair Fitter, 1987.)

FOR DAN

Contents

Prologue

TRÀIGH LAR BEACH IS a small machair beach at the end of Horgabost Sands on the west coast of the Isle of Harris in the Outer Hebrides of northern Scotland. *Machair* is the name given to the flat western coastal plain of Harris, its beaches made of the shells and skeletons of ancient sea creatures ground to fine sand by the ceaseless pounding of the ocean. Breakers roll in with the roar of an oncoming train, leaving drainage channels in pale blue-green gold and symmetrical ripple marks above the high-tide line. Accumulated sand forms wide white beaches and bordering dunes. Calcium limes the dark acidic peat soils behind into rich fertile grassland.

Standing on Tràigh Lar Beach, you can hardly feel more solitary, more lulled by its stark beauty and breathtaking peace. Black birds shoot in and out of nooks in the ancient rock walls that line the road to Tarbert. Seagulls and carrion crows hang motionless in the air. Cuckoos call from groves of stunted trees, and hawks soar with ravens.

Flotsam, carried on the Gulf Stream from the New World, has tangled in the seaweed on Tràigh Lar, dotting the shimmering sand. During the summer months, the machair lining its borders is adorned with a blanket of wildflowers.

Erica

*Heather, a low-growing perennial shrub that dominates the heathlands, moors, and acidic peat bogs of Europe, was often called **Erica**—Calluna vulgaris—in traditional references. Not a true heather, Erica's mauve flowers bloom on the machair in the spring.*

RODEL, ISLE OF HARRIS,
OUTER HEBRIDES, SCOTLAND,
OCTOBER 3

The wide-faced clock over the bar here at the Rodel Hotel moves backwards. Three o'clock in the morning posts as 9:00 p.m. I'm comforted by that, buoyed by the steady procession of hours and minutes piling up in front of me.

On a fluke, my recent novella, *Remembrance and Mania*, just won the faintly prestigious Comstock Award for short fiction. As a consequence, I've had a two-book contract flung across my shoulders like a length of chain mail.

I'm stagnant with fear.

I'm empty, deficient, inept.

I've nothing to say and no words to say it with.

We've just settled into our self-catering cottage in Rodel, at the southern tip of Harris, after a seven-hour drive from Glasgow to Uig on the Isle of Skye, with my husband, Greyson, at the wheel. We took the ferry across the Minch to Tarbert this morning.

In our rental car then, in the wind and the rain, we sailed to Rodel on the eastern shore single-track Finsbay road. Harris had once conjoined with the Scottish mainland but had slipped into the sea at the end of the last ice age. Waterlogged bogs and black tarns lay about at every turn, stabbed with the sharp bony intrusions of gray gneiss.

The evening before our Glasgow flight, I'd offered up a thin slice of my soul in gratitude at the annual Comstock Awards banquet in London.

"A book of towering achievement, equal parts critique and passion," Tawny Woodhouse, Comstock's ebullient director, pronounced on introducing "our grand prize winner."

And though I broach neither process nor achievement with any ease, Comstock left me spunky and bold. I soared as though that gold-embossed curlicued certificate—"*Erica Winchat, First Place, Short Fiction*"—had given me wings. Wings now clipped by my own feelings of inadequacy.

❧

RODEL, HARRIS,
OCTOBER 4

I woke up last night at about two o'clock. No moon, no stars, and I could barely see my hand in front of my face. Outside the bedroom window, the land and the sky stretched off in a forever coal-blackness, just one shade darker than my own shriveled psyche. I'm a fraud. I know that now. I can't possibly write anything of substance ever again. But Greyson won't let me wallow in it.

Late this afternoon, we sloshed through an old peat cutting bog just off the Finsbay road. At the seaward end, we climbed a hillock to watch storm-tossed waves heave themselves at the cliff base below. Black-headed gulls hovered above, and a brown-eyed fulmar exulted with two consecutive flybys within arm's reach.

About a third of a mile further on, a rock cairn marked the site of a crippled broch-like tower, its stone walls now reduced to a heap of rubble covered in thin brown grass. And on the margins of the peat bog, at the far end of a small black pool, stood a ruined croft filled with gravelly mounds of dirt and old wire. Its yawning windows trumpeted a forlorn emptiness.

Someone had lived there once, in veiled optimism. Or, perhaps more likely, smothered in despair.

Over a game of pool last night, the Rodel Hotel barkeep had told us the story of Donald MacDonald and his betrothed, Jessie of Balranald. In 1850, young Donald—too forgiving of the estate's crofters—had been dismissed as assistant factor in North Uist, an island to the south of Harris. Jessie's father pressed her to marry Donald's mean-spirited successor, but Jessie declined, and she and Donald set off for the Isle of Skye. A storm-tossed night forced their ship back to Tarbert where Jessie's brother seized the couple and imprisoned them in Rodel House—now the Rodel Hotel. They escaped out a window in the Red Room and made their way to Australia.

Surely even *I* could structure something warm and sentient from such poignancy.

THE LOCHBOISDALE HOTEL, LOCHBOISDALE, SOUTH UIST, OUTER HEBRIDES, SCOTLAND, OCTOBER 5

We're in our room, looking out across the rolling Minch to Canna and Rum. We off-loaded in Otternish on North Uist and drove south, arriving here just short of five o'clock.

After breakfast at the Anchorage this morning, a Leverburgh restaurant dressed in honey-colored pine, we sailed on the MV *Loch Bhrusda* ferry to North Uist. No ship was scheduled for that time, but "sometimes the ferry just shows up," our waitress, Siobhan, said. Alert to the slightest shift on the horizon, she'd spotted the black dot approach of the *Bhrusda* well before anyone else.

For forty-five minutes then, the small boat beat against the wind and the waves through one of the loneliest stretches of the planet I've ever seen. Distant black islands dulled with the rain. Plumes of spray nibbled at their base. But sometimes, like the bright flash of a dream, sunlight shimmered on the heaving sea.

The low groan of grinding engines, undertones humming like an oncoming tank, sang above a frigid wind. Except for the driver of a BP oil truck, who very quickly vanished, Greyson and I were the ferry's only passengers. No one manned the bridge either, that we could see. If I could just rouse my imagination long enough to create something compelling from that.

THE LOCHMADDY HOTEL, LOCHMADDY, NORTH UIST, OCTOBER 6

We left Lochboisdale just after breakfast. One of the most intriguing things about the hotel there was a carved cherrywood armchair that stood in the hallway, all loops and sculpted lyres. Though it had been there "forever," no one could tell us where it had come from. And what about that Kilbride Shellfish truck abandoned just below the Neolithic chambered tomb of Minngearraidh on Reineval Hill. How did *that* get there?

Back here on North Uist, we negotiated a short, potholed road to Langass Lodge, waiting in the car in a light rain as a middle-aged Aussie couple walked their long-haired Siamese, Skye, up and around the stone circle of Pobull Fhinn.

RODEL, HARRIS,
OCTOBER 7

At breakfast this morning in Lochmaddy, they played oldies from the fifties and sixties, and Greyson and I had a slow dance to Roy Orbison's "Crying." How apropos for my numbed and moldering spirit.

On the way back to the Otternish-Tarbert ferry, we lingered at Dun an Sticir, another ruined broch in a small back tarn. Broken walls stood ten feet high in places, and the remnants of a stone causeway lay visible just under the surface of the pond's crystalline water. Of course, we slogged on over in our wellies, as fog slid down off the tops of the hills and three white swans cruised the loch like the spirits of long-gone tenants.

RODEL, HARRIS,
OCTOBER 8

Stories as thick as clotted cream spring out of these Harris peat bogs. The church next door, for instance, St. Clement's, dates back to the sixteenth century. Effigies of medieval knights, set in the interior walls and bordered with Celtic knots, offer no shortage of possibilities.

And sheep. Sheep stand everywhere. Never troubled by wind or rain, they idle in roadways, oblivious to oncoming traffic, finally moving off, paunchy Tribble bodies on spindly legs. If the incessant wind were somehow sapped of its energy, grinding sheep jaws would fill the void.

Later on, just up from some glassy loch off a skinny interior byway, we stumbled on an overturned lorry lying in the peaty muck. A half dozen young people, most of them with Cockney accents, had gathered round in cable-knit sweaters, blue jeans, and Wellington boots, and collectively, we helped them work an old upright piano fallen from the van onto a flatbed truck. Who was moving to such wilds from England?

❦

RODEL, HARRIS,
OCTOBER 9

Greyson and I played golf at the Isle of Harris Golf Course this morning. Two congenial Scotsmen, on playing the third tee, lent us their clubs. Between intermittent rain squalls, loitering sheep, and rabbit-warren sand traps, we finished a solid round, the sea a thundering backdrop.

I've been scouting the wide white sands of West Harris for inspiration. Flat and firm, they're overflown by hawks and ravens. The marram-grass dunes and plains behind are called machair, pocked with rabbit holes and patches of cultivated grains, small sheaves tied up with straw. Redshanks bob among the wildflowers.

Just to the west of Seilebost Sands, the farthest machair from Rodel, lies our favorite beach—Tràigh Lar. Tràigh (pronounced "try") is Gaelic for *sandy*, and Lar means *floor*. When the sea is wild and blue, Tràigh Lar is astonishing. Even with high tide, waves continue to shatter on Tràigh Lar in a frothy mass.

To the left, the empty Toe Head peninsula extends three miles into the Atlantic, capped by the moorish hill of Chaipaval, and joined to the mainland by a strip of machair, with a sandy beach to either side. The island of Taransay lies to the right. And between them—emptiest of all—are the distant deserted islands of St. Kilda. On the hillside above Tràigh Lar, the MacLeod Stone rises tall and thin, one face covered in crusty pale-blue lichen.

We wandered back to the roadway through blankets of limpet shells deposited in a tangle of seaweed and flotsam. A cigarette lighter, a jar of pickled onions, the handle of a child's bucket, an empty ketchup holder, a rock-concert laminate badge, a green plastic laundry basket, a packet of arthritis pills . . .

Now where did these come from?

Melody Rose

(An Empty Ketchup Holder)

*White Common Eyebright–Eurphrasia nemorosa–
latches its roots onto nearby plants for sustenance.*

HE HAD A FACE LIKE polished driftwood. Sculpted. Ageless. So fluid and graceful, it was almost courtly. When he danced, his thin old-man arms dangled at his sides and he shuffled across the pavement on crimped legs. Someone from the stage, without looking, called him "Pops."

"Give it a rest, will ya, Pops?"

But the old man's name was Walker, and some of them up there knew it.

Old Walker crooked a finger at a little boy in red passing by—a chubby all-smiles toddler in an oversized baseball cap and bare, dirty feet. "One small dance, eh, big fella?" He dropped down, bent almost double, wagged a bony finger in the boy's face, and winked. "Oh, come on now." His voice rasped like a file over the music from the stage, and he coiled the finger over his palm. Once. Twice.

All afternoon, the little boy in red had circled the seated

folk-festival crowd, wobbling haphazardly up this side and down the other under the attentive but distant eye of his father. Now, in front of the old man, he lurched to a halt and stared at the creased and empty outstretched hand. His hazelnut eyes gleamed like buffed sandalwood, and he worked his small pink mouth into an extravagant pout.

"Jason!" The boy pitched forward with the sound of a coarse male voice from out of the crowd. "Jason!"

Jason pulled a stubby arm from behind his back and thrust it toward the old man just as his father, a craggy young man in tattered Levi's and a stale blue T-shirt, swooped in and plucked the child away.

"Time to go, sport," he said, hoisting the little boy up into the air, where he hung over his father's head, suspended by two freckled arms. And then, vicelike, his chunky baby-fat legs clamped to left and right on the man's shoulders.

"Time to go, sport," his father said again. And, without a single glance at the old man, he lumbered off into the crowd like a freighter putting out to sea.

Old Walker unfolded his bones in the manner of old men everywhere and swayed over the concrete slab fronting the stage, like an empty skiff in a sea breeze. Above him, a dark-haired, pasty-faced man in a ruby-red cotton T-shirt and thick black-rimmed glasses stepped forward to introduce the next act.

"If y'all are lucky"—and the old man was not—"you saw this next group at Voodoo Mama's last Saturday night," the man on stage announced.

A rowdy wave of approval rippled through the crowd as three booted and bearded young men with instruments of a bluegrass nature strolled to the center of the stage.

"Please welcome, from right here in Orleans Parish, New Orleans's very own Catfish Bayou String Band."

Almost at once, the three men in boots and beards began to harmonize, their melodies reflecting on earthly goods, dire straits, and destitution, followed by a splattering of faith, duty, and good conscience. All of these the people heard with intense appreciation, and they nodded to one another with doleful eyes, their lips pursed.

Up against the great river, behind the French Market, a tent for the hungry and the homeless, the blamed and the unseen, had been set up by the festival's management. Long-haired young men passed by in tattered shoes, with grimy sleeping bags strapped to their backs; old men the color of raw coal, wrapped in woolen overcoats and wearing greasy hobnailed boots. A young woman in a broadly flowered peasant dress, with the timeless expression of the luckless, hauled along three ratty boy children with pinched faces, ankle-high trousers, and a bitter but drowsy resignation. The people ignored all of these, as the wind ignores the trees.

Old Walker rocked back on his heels, cradled his gray-white head, and swayed over the pavement. He was so old now. So broken.

"You've got the second-best dry goods shop in town here," the old man's friend, Arley, had told him, twenty years ago now. But the fisheries had closed, and then the market, followed in short order by hearts and minds. And of course, the second-best had gone first.

Under the arched gray brush of his eyebrows, Old Walker's chestnut eyes brimmed with tears, and the hollows of his cheeks sunk further. He covered his lost face with lost hands and began to moan to the rhythm from the stage.

Mardi Gras swirled around the plaza, aglow with springtime. Crepe paper flowers bordering the stage—lemon yellow, deep purple, and a satiny pea green—fluttered in the cool breeze that slipped in from the Mississippi.

❧

UP AGAINST THE edge of the cement block where the old man rested, sagged, for no apparent reason, a battered, gray-metal table. And alternately hunched under the table, starched and stiff on top of the table, and wrapped around the legs of the table, fiddled a lanky all-bone child of seven or eight named Melody Rose . . . Melody Rose Beckman.

"Melody Rose Beckman . . . that's not yours!"

"Melody Rose Beckman . . . act your age!"

"Melody Rose Beckman . . . stay out of there!"

"Melody Rose Beckman . . . leave the baby alone!"

Melody Rose Beckman's mother flew about everywhere and nowhere, like one of those big-belled, wide-eyed smiling alarm clocks that race around on old Saturday morning cartoons. Only Melody Rose Beckman's mother, slim and slight of face and form, never smiled. There was no time. In her lap, she bounced a boy baby, plump and prattling. For him she cooed on occasion and waggled her face in his face in the exaggerated fashion of mothers everywhere.

The baby hacked and heaved a load of soured milk over the mother's silky blouse, and so Melody Rose's mother called out yet again: "Melody Rose Beckman, get out from under there. You ruin that dress, and you'll never see another one."

Melody Rose slithered out to sit cross-legged on a drain cover beside the table. Brushing grass from her pale-green sundress, she fingered her brother's baby bottle in one pocket. The knobs on the drain cover's metal lid stamped a squared pattern along the backs of her thin legs. Her blond pigtails, colored as if a mixture of angel wings and sunlight, dropped further down her shoulders as she watched her mother pull a string of rubbery toys from the baby's stroller. One by one, her mother offered these to him. And one by one, the baby gurgled and spit and threw them all away.

Not so long ago, Melody Rose remembered, life was different. Her mother had said things to her like, "Melody Rose, sing me that pretty little song . . . You know, the one you learned in school . . . about the inch worm," or, "Just look at you, Melody Rose. What a big girl you're getting to be."

In those days, Melody Rose Beckman's mother had almost always smiled. There was time. But now her mother was demanding, "Melody Rose Beckman . . . get that baby bottle back here . . . right now!"

And Melody Rose did. She chewed on her lower lip in the process and grimaced and made faces into the ground and the grass. And once she even stuck her tongue out at the baby—from behind her mother's back. But she fetched the baby's bottle from a deep pocket of her sunflowered skirt and walked it over to her mother.

In the end, of course, there was a bottle for Melody Rose too—a red plastic ketchup bottle filled with sugar water. The bottle top planted between her thin tight lips, Melody Rose swooshed back and forth across the concrete slab behind the baby-empty stroller, in front of the stage and the crumpled old man, moving ever further and further away from her mother.

From out of the milling crowd by the po'boy stand, a young girl popped up, just a year or so past Melody Rose's age, only far plumper. Her brothers—two of them—were playing in the parking lot, the girl said. That left her all alone.

"I can push your buggy, too, and we can be friends," the older girl said, clamping a hand on the smooth black crossbar of the baby's hefty, padded buggy.

A saddle of freckles marched across the bridge of the older girl's nose. Her two sharp, ice-colored eyes settled, not on Melody Rose Beckman, but instead on the contents of the buggy—fuzz-faced toys and undershirts, rubber teething rings and throwaway diapers.

Melody Rose's bright eyes quickened and narrowed. "They're not mine," she said, looking at the girl sideways from under her thick black lashes. "They're my baby brother's. He's over there." Melody Rose pointed a skinny pink arm in the direction of her mother.

The bigger girl grinned and shoved the buggy forward while Melody Rose's free hand slid down, seized the closest angle of the black handle, and jerked back. Hardly together, they started off toward the low oil-splattered cement steps dropping down to the river. Melody Rose tossed her plastic bottle in the direction of the buggy, but it grazed the handlebars, bounced just once on the grass, and slipped forever into the river. She knew at once that she'd never see anything like that bottle—her very own—ever again.

"Melody Rose, get back from that river, right now!" her mother ordered. And, of course, Melody Rose did.

IN THE PATCH of grass beside the audience, between Melody Rose's drain cover and the table, there poked upward, two or three inches, the loop of an open drain pipe. Unaware of its presence, passersby stumbled here almost as a matter of course. Whenever they did, Melody Rose's mother half smiled despite her weariness, and her peppery eyes flickered as a dead gull's wing might flutter in a breeze. She bounced the baby more exuberantly in her lap.

Each and every time, the people noticed only with a dull embarrassment. And, of course, none of them ever really looked. This time though, when the old man fell as he passed—or maybe because the old man fell—everyone muttered just a little louder.

WALKER MEANT ONLY to sit down, to stretch out. Maybe even to nap by the wall of the stage. But he'd snagged a shoe on a pipe-stem's upper lip and went down with the whimper of a wounded puppy. He righted himself and forced his back up against a tree trunk set firmly in the spring-soft grass. By chance, his tired old-man eyes met the sad fawn-colored ones of the broken-faced little girl who'd scooted away the last hour or so behind her baby brother's overloaded stroller. She alone—Melody Rose Beckman—had allowed herself to see him.

The little girl stood apart from the crowd, back to the peeled-paint rails of the incline to the river. A second child, older, now possessed the buggy, and this pudgy girl swung up and down the pavement, in endless and ever-widening circles.

Walker hauled himself to his feet again, and with all the quiet dignity he could muster, he ambled across to where the little girl waited. On stage, the latest attraction charmed the crowd with dulcimer and fiddle and tambourine. Something tuneful and agreeable and safe, about better days and yesterday being gone. And didn't we all know it.

The old man took the little girl's slivered hands into his own, and they danced. They danced with short shuffling steps, with a pure sort of wordless joy. Eyes shining. All smiles. Like fragments of broken colored glass glittering in the sunlight. Like fallen leaves twirling in an errant summer breeze.

And then Melody Rose Beckman's mother stood up with the baby and called out, without looking, "Melody Rose Beckman! Bring me the baby's buggy. It's time to go home."

So Melody Rose Beckman dropped the old man's hands and watched the light in his eyes fade. And then she was gone.

Brook

(A Packet of Arthritis Pills)

Creamy spikes of **Brook***weed–Samolus valerandi–a plant once used to counteract blood poisoning, spring from creeping underground stems.*

THIS IS JEANINE COHEN. She reminds me of my grandmother. That pale, almost translucent roundish face, the lashless eyes, those thin colorless lips. See the vague upturn at the corner of her mouth, the way she looks like she's almost smiling? There's a sort of peace in that. Like she's rising above a bad dream, a forgetfulness. I think they'd all like to do that, don't you? I mean forget about life. Just get out. Mrs. Cohen's been here since two weeks ago last Friday. Final tortured stages of cervical cancer. She'll be gone soon.

My grandmother had an aneurysm in her abdomen. She went fast. But before they let her go, they'd sit her up in a chair in the nursing home—two days before she died. And they *made* her eat. God awful, don't you think? This woman rode horses when she was eighty, and went solo trekking to Bhutan. She couldn't even pee or lift a fork anymore. But they put her in that chair and they *made* her eat.

That was almost ten years ago now. I was only nine or

ten, but I remember going into the room with my mother and seeing Grandma propped up in one of those god-awful chairs with the little iron wheels? Her eyes were black slits. I don't think she knew who I was. But she looked up when I came in, and there was this kind of plea on her face. I'll never forget it.

Mrs. Cohen here's nearly eighty-eight. She's had a good, long life, I think. Ending it shouldn't be such a trial or an ordeal. I'm giving it a lot of thought. Wouldn't you?

My mom and dad used to take us down to visit Grandma when we were little, at least once a year, down to Delhi by Lake Erie. Toronto was just too sprawling for her. She said she got hives, but I don't think so. I mean, Bhutan's no picnic. It's farm country down there, you know.

Delhi, I mean. She went there to cool her heels between adventures, she used to say. I always stayed at her house when everyone else was across the road at my uncle's. She had a pump in her kitchen. Can you believe it? A pump. In the kitchen. And pillow cases she embroidered herself. I could feel the bumps from the stitching on my fingers at night. We used to play cribbage, and she'd fix me warm milk before I went to bed, heated on her woodstove. I slept a lot better down there than I ever did at home. My mom just didn't have the time for that. Never did. Still doesn't, I guess.

I've worked here nearly two years now, and I always learn a lot from these old ladies. Take Mrs. Bellevue down the hall in 3llC. What good is it to anybody to have her lying there incontinent and blind? She's got Alzheimer's, and I mean *real* bad. Didn't know who I was the other day. Told me she wanted to go home. Back to Pittsburgh. Teach piano again. Well, I knew what she meant. Don't we all? Want to go home, I mean. Who wants to feel like their brains are being sucked out, you know what I mean?

I was in there last night and watched her a long time in

the dark. She looked like a corpse, all swathed up in white cotton sheets, stinking like old lady, bedsores and urine. She opened her eyes once, and I saw this awful blankness there, like she was some half-dead animal caught in a trap. My grandmother had that same hopelessness on her face.

The woman that was in that room before her—Celia Martin, I think it was—she had that same horrid look just before she went. I mean, it was a real blessing when her oxygen failed.

Before I came here, I worked two years in the emergency room at Sick Kids. We had some real close calls there. It took a toll on everyone. It's not easy being the one who watches them all suffer. I mean, doctors come and doctors go and even the RNs. A shot here, a shot there, lay out the meds, bark out the orders. But we CNAs, we do all of the grunt work. We're the ones up close and personal, changing the bedpans and the diapers, cleaning butts and bedsores. Somebody's gotta do it.

My mom couldn't even be on the ward without going all squishy. Queasy-like. *What a burden for families to have children in such a state,* she always said. She had a hard enough time of it with us normal kids. I remember once, when we were all under eight—there's four of us, me, my older sister, Mandy, and the twins, Cara and Crystal—she took us to the park and left us there. At least that's how I remember it. I mean, she was gone for hours.

Mandy told me years later that she'd gone to meet some boyfriend, some sailor, 'cause Dad was on the road. He was some kind of salesman. Insurance, I think. Anyway, he was gone all the time. That's all I remember. I don't believe her though. Mandy, I mean. Moms don't do that sort of thing, do they? Leave their kids alone. Well, no, I'm not that big a baby. But *my* mom wouldn't do it, eh? Grandma wouldn't have done it . . .

Jane Harris here had a massive stroke in a nursing home about a week ago. Skinny as a bean, she is. Can't even eat on her own anymore. They feed her with a tube. She's a mess any which way you look at it. Her family can't seem to see their way to cutting off her food and water. But she shouldn't have to lie around here like that much longer. Not if I can help it.

Grandma was poorly in the end, too, of course. We didn't go down to see her as much as we used to. I don't know why, really. Maybe it was just too much trouble for Mom. Probably. I mean, Grandma was in and out of the hospital and then into that god-awful nursing home.

She told me once that I should look into nursing. *All that blond hair of yours, Brook*, she'd say. *You'd look good in white*. Ha! Like that's any part of it, eh? But I *do* look good in white. I don't go much for all those colored scrubs with dogs and cats and balloons and seashells and teddy bears. That kind of shit. Unprofessional, I think. I mean, white has a purity to it, don't you think? You can keep your distance in white. It's clean. It's simple. It's straightforward. The color of truth, I think. There's black. And then there's white.

When I first finished my CNA training I thought, well, yeah, now I can do my bit to help make people's lives a bit easier, you know. But it doesn't happen that way much, at least it doesn't for me. But I think now, that as long as there's so much pain in healing, I'd see about making those hurting a bit more whole again in some way. You know what I mean? Not just slapping on a gauze bandage or swabbing dry lips. I can make the inevitable easier on everyone, less of a torment. Hospice work is really satisfying that way.

Take Mrs. Samolus next door. She's one of my favorites. She was brought here from a convalescent home outside of Drayton. She's ninety-two. And bedsores? How nice can that be, eh? We have to turn her two, maybe three times a day, when we can get around to it. We've got a lot on our plates, you know. See here on her chart? They've prescribed arthritis pills? Arthritis pills! Can you imagine? You're gorked out in some steel-armed bed in a room full of nothing, unless you count the god-awful drone of that iron-lung oxygen machine over there. And they're worried about arthritis?

I took the last packet of pills with me on a picnic to Toronto Island with my boyfriend, Pierce. We've been going out since senior high. Pierce is okay for the time being. But he's junk, really, on the nerdy side. You know what I mean? All these idiot puns flying out of his face morning and night. I aim to snag me a doctor in time, no doubt about it. Don't laugh.

Anyway, Pierce has a kinda cruel way about him at times. Like we were making our way to the back of the island, and I don't know if you've been there or not, but they have these signs, "Please Walk on the Grass," eh? I think that's awesome, so I'm just about to head across. We're going to the other side anyway, where the paddleboats are. And old Pierce has this all-out hissy fit. If everybody did that there'd be no grass at all. Yadda, yadda, yadda. That kind of shit. Well, that's just stupid. Why put a sign like that up if you don't mean it? So anyway, we walked way the hell around. But I was telling him about old Mrs. Samolus, and he got all frothy and worked up about those arthritis pills. Said I needed to take them back. The docs wouldn't have given them to her if they weren't doing some good. Blah, blah, blah.

Well, let me tell you, I've seen plenty in that place that's not doing anybody a damn shot of good. Making those old ladies' lives more miserable than they already are. Ha! Good thing I didn't bring up oxygen machines, eh? When old

Pierce wasn't looking, I tossed those pills into the lake. And that's the last we'll see of them.

So anyway, this is Mrs. Janus. She's gonna go soon too. I just know it.

Ella

(An Artificial Lotus Blossom)

Prunella grandiflora or Self-heal, a low-growing plant with whorls of two-lipped purple flowers on dense spikes, has antibacterial and antiseptic properties. In the early days, it was commonly used as an herbal tonic.

THAT DITZY BLONDE IN those gauzy harem pants, she's got a peace symbol on her vest, I'm guessing. She smells like patchouli and some kind of herbal tea. A pungent peppermint. Maybe lemongrass. She'll be in full lotus position like an anemic pretzel. I'll just sneak a peek.

Yeah. I thought so.

I can haul in the sole of one foot so it's up against my thigh. But if I bring the left foot in, too, my knee's gonna pop up to the ceiling like a capsized dinghy.

Okay—that's enough. It's just a twenty-minute meditation.

Breathe in. Breathe out.

Breathe in. Breathe out.

Let go . . . Relax.

Focus on the breath.

Inhale—and exhale.

Inhale—and exhale.

If I'd just set the alarm for seven o'clock instead of giving myself only fifteen minutes to get here from the hotel, I wouldn't be sitting up here right in front of the stage looking pathetic, needy and adoring. Tomorrow I'll snag a seat way at the back.

When your stomach growls, how far does a sound like that travel?

Okay—okay—just breathe.

Breathe in. Breathe out.

Breathe in. Breathe out.

Inhale—and exhale.

Inhale.

And exhale.

That ditzy blonde's name probably isn't really Kenisha either. Kenisha . . . Kenesha. Whatever. She looks Scandinavian with all that bleached-blond hair. When we opened this session, she grabbed that mic like it was the baton in a relay race. Nearly took out my eardrums. "Can you hear me? Can you hear me?" Some people just like to hear themselves talk. Especially if there's a recorder somewhere. Even if it's just a smartphone.

But this is big stuff. Eric Decker up there is one of the top meditation gurus in the country. We're lucky to have him. He's gonna make some serious money on this thing in the end. How much does he clear for a gig like this anyway, I wonder?

A "little bit more about boundaries," that Barbie-doll Kenisha wanted to know. How to deal with "strong negative emotions . . . expanding demographics." Like, "How can we illuminate the relationship between intention and allowing?" Do people make this stuff up? What the hell does that mean anyway?

I'm guessing she can't stand her husband anymore. They're in the middle of a messy divorce, and she wants someone to tell her what to do and how to do it.

Me too, maybe. Do I? I guess it depends on what I'd be doing. I know for sure I'd like to be doing anything else right about now.

My butt's gone numb already.

Okay. That's it. Relax! Relax!

Just breathe.

Focus on the breath.

In—and out.

In—and out.

That ponytailed hanger-on up there on stage nodded the whole time Barbie was babbling. Bobble-head. Bubble-head. Bobble-head. He looked like that lame doll we picked up for Lacy Blue on her third birthday. Or was it her fourth? Four? Five? The hair wasn't as long. And it was mud red. Auburn. Maybe auburn. Is auburn brown or red?

Auburn University. Alabama, I think. Redneck Alabamans. So. Auburn. Red?

Huh.

A few more friends could have popped over for Lacy Blue's party that year. Does it break little baby hearts to be neglected like that? Does stuff like that stay around in a kid's psyche? I mean, is she gonna remember that shit when she's fifty years old?

I did like the way that neo-hippie on the other side of Barbie there rubbed her back. She's "learning to embrace opportunity," she said. It's a struggle. She's wrestling it to the ground right now. A big sucker, opportunity is. A sumo wrestler slathered up in coconut oil, wearing one of those little white diapers. On the count of ten then—and you're out!

Ten!

It's gotta be at least ten minutes by now. I'd peek at my watch, but Eric's gonna be ogling me if I do. I bet *his* eyes aren't necessarily shut tight when he's meditating. Checking out the ladies, Eric?

Hell, I'm gonna peek. My eyes are just slits. He'll never see.

No way! Five minutes! I didn't think time could crawl this slow. I'm gonna have to scratch my nose. Who's gonna notice?

Okay! Cut it out now.

Take a deep breath.

In—and out.

In—and out.

Meditation shouldn't be so damn hard. Just watch your thoughts, they say. If they're headed for the door . . . well, maybe. And who's "they" anyway? "They" say this. "They" say that.

Oh, look! Here comes a thought now. What does a thought look like anyway? Are some thoughts skinny, like starved cats? Are some thoughts Chris Christie–sized, like gigantic hot-air balloons? So, there's Laurel and Hardy thoughts then? This thought I'm watching now is shifty-eyed and slithery. Hangs out on street corners with greasy hair, smoking pot.

Maybe meditation's just one more avoidance strategy. Ever thought of that, Eric? What makes this new book of yours so special anyway?

They all do it, these gurus and swamis. Pen some massive volume about knowing and not knowing, grounding this and expanding that. Is that like grinding broken glass under your bootheel? And what about expanding waistlines?

I scarfed up Eric's last effort, *Embracing Change*, right out of the gate. "Hearing in a deep way," the cover blurb of this new one says. What does that mean anyway? And how deep is deep? Are we talking under water? Under ground? The Underground? Meditating on the London Tube?

It's got to be fifteen minutes by now. Twenty minutes is a lifetime! I don't think I'm gonna live that long.

Damn it! That's enough now.

Breathe in.

Breathe out.

Relax.

Just watch the breath.

Let it go. Let it all go.

Take it all off.

Was that Gypsy Rose Lee? I don't remember.

Seems you were more about embracing your personal assistant, the comely Katelyn, eh, Eric? Wife's left you then, has she? I think we can all see how adoringly Ms. K looks at you. You're only human after all. Nothing lasts forever, even in guru-dom.

Had us all stand and stretch while you figured out where you were in your notes. Were we at that bit about "the reality of impermanence"? Were we "taking comfort in groundlessness"? Or was it all about "holding our options with a greater capacity"?

Blah, blah, blah.

It's a long drive up here from Boston. I've never seen the coast of Maine before. Nice. Pretty gnarly up this way in the winter, I'll bet. Nice spot for a retreat though, especially here in Bar Harbor.

We could maybe slide on up for a mini-vacation sometime. Lacy Blue would love it. I can hear Kenny now though. "Ella, Ella, Ella," he's gonna say, like always. "We're not made of money, girl. Maine's summer people and winter people. We're neither."

Okay. Okay. That's enough? Let it go.

We're right here. We're right now.

Breathe. Breathe.

Inhale.

And exhale.

God, I'm hungry!

When's he gonna tap that damn brass bowl again and end this bloody session? Sounds like a tuberculosis ward in here, all the hacking and coughing. Somebody's cell phone's gonna go off any minute now.

Kinda nice to see Abigail made it this far north. I wonder why she didn't message me or post anything on Facebook. We could have carpooled or something.

Wish we wouldn't have had that silent break mid-morning. I forgot and spoke to Abbey in the line for the ladies and she glared at me for breaking the silence like I'd just called her mother a whore. You can't apologize for something like that either. I just waved my hands in her face, mouthed *I'm sorry,* and then gave her one of those long hugs everyone dishes out in these circles. Checked my watch over her shoulder just to make sure I held on long enough. Twenty seconds, on the nose!

"We're growing into a new way of being."

"We're moving on, through and upward."

"Our authentic, intuitive selves know exactly how to be in this world."

Maybe I'll snag that fake purply lotus blossom Eric's got floating up there in his brandy snifter. Take it back for Lacy Blue. Someone else nicked the one from yesterday's session. Same size. Same color. I saw it floating off the pier last night.

Robin

(The Handle of a Child's Bucket)

*Coral-pink Ragged **Robin**—Silene flos-cuculi—has deeply divided petals.*

From: Tcampion@supernet.com
To: Slogan@supernet.com
Subject: Robin

Hello Shanty,
As you can appreciate, it's been an unimaginably tough summer. The first since Robin's death. I know you've been asked so many times already, even in a criminal capacity I suspect, but I would appreciate hearing any and all details of that awful night yet again.

I just can't reconcile the fact that Robin never mentioned you in all the months you were seeing each other. It's so unlike her. We were very close, as I'm sure you know. You were too old for her, and I wish you would have discouraged her interest. Made her realize that at fifteen she was far too young for any serious relationship, especially with someone nearly twenty years old.

You're as familiar with the environs of Robert's Arm and beyond as anyone, and working for Biff Leinoff's logging crew must have required you to drive that road to

Corner Brook many times before. So why were you speeding? Why did you have Robin out so late on a school night in the first place? All reasoning escapes me.

Please help me to understand why your life goes on as ever when Robin's is no more and any peace for me has been utterly shattered.

I've attached a photo of Robin's junior high graduation last fall. All lace and ribbons she was, as you can see. Blue was her favorite color. It brought out the sea colors in her eyes. A sweet, sweet child she was. So full of promise and possibility. An innocent life snuffed out just like that on one of our lonely Newfoundland byways.

I hope to hear from you.

Sincerely,
Tilda Campion

From: Slogan@supernet.com
To: Tcampion@supernet.com
Subject: Robin

Dear Mrs. Campion,
I can only say that it was beyond devastating for me to wake up in the Stephensville Hospital last April and be told that Robin was gone! It still seems unreal to me.

We really hadn't been seeing each other at all. Robin was my sister, Carla's, best friend, as you know, and I guess it was inevitable that we'd get to know each other somewhat.

I have to say, once again, that I don't remember much of that night at all, except for the thick fog that still seems to smother everything about it. I don't even know for sure when we set off for home, or even any friends we might have seen in town.

I'm so sorry for the loss of your daughter and for whatever part I played in it. I am, it seems, very much at fault, though accepting blame can never be enough, I know. How could it be? If I could say or do anything to ease your pain, I would do it gladly. I know you will never be able to forgive me. I will never forgive myself.

    Sincerely,

    Shanty Logan

From: Tcampion@supernet.com
To: Slogan@supernet.com
Subject: Robin

Shanty,

Accidents like this can diminish one's memory, I know. But surely there's something, however trivial, that you can bring to mind. It would mean the world to me to be able to somehow align myself with Robin in her final hours. Regrettably, I'm torn with the injustice of her life being snatched away from me, while yours, spared for whatever reason, goes on as usual. Your suffering is great, I have no doubt. But there is no way it can possibly compare to a mother's loss of her only child.

    I have so little of Robin's essence with me now. Somewhere I read of a man who kept a beach ball filled with a loved one's breath, his wife's, I think. Someone who'd been lost to him. I have nothing along those lines beyond a lock of Robin's hair, a soft sand-colored swatch from the day she was born.

    There are, of course, simpler items, like the cobalt-blue toothbrush she never managed to get back in the holder. It's still lying on the bathroom counter where she left it all those many months ago. That's all I have. Beyond an infinity of memories that play continually in my head, always coming to rest, if that's the right word, on her bruised and broken body.

    I have attached here an old snapshot taken down by the harbor when she was about three years old. We'd only just lost her father to cancer. I hardly ever go out anymore, and so I've buried myself in old photographs these past months, as something of an escape. This one caught my eye. That oversized cap she's wearing, I guess.

I had only just remarked the morning of the accident that she looked quite piqued, as though she'd lost sleep a night or two. Her eyes were hollow and dark. She shrugged me off and set off for Central High as usual. Carla was waiting by the bus stop. I could see her from the kitchen window. I know, of course, that Carla was with you and Robin that awful night, but she has thus far refused to talk to me.

That was the last I ever saw of my darling girl. You can't imagine what that has done to me. So I feel certain that there's something, however mundane, that you can add to that day. Perhaps you owe it to Robin's memory?

Sincerely,
Tilda Campion

From: Slogan@supernet.com
To: Tcampion@supernet.com
Subject: Robin

Dear Mrs. Campion,

I will try again to give you as accurate an account of that night as I can. As I've said, I fetched the girls from school to drive down to Corner Brook for a Harry Martin concert. That stretch of road is a lonely one at the best of times, and a dense fog had rolled in by the time we headed for home. I don't now recall the exact time, but it had to be close to midnight, maybe later.

We weren't dating, Mrs. Campion, and if Robin implied otherwise, I don't know how she got that idea. I never led her on in any way. Carla can vouch for that. It was my understanding that Robin had your okay for this trip, so I can only say that I'm sorry I didn't follow up on that.

After the concert, we started directly for home. Moose always seem to find that stretch of road, so I can tell you, without hesitation, that I was not speeding. I just have no other specific recollection of what happened on the drive.

I only remember waking up in Stephensville, or it may have been Port aux Basques, days later. I wish I could help you in some way through this terrible loss. Maybe one day you will find it in your heart to forgive me.

Sincerely,
Shanty

From: Tcampion@supernet.com
To: Slogan@supernet.com
Subject: Robin

Shanty,
There may well come a day for forgiveness, though that's not an option for me at present, I'm afraid. There are days when I can barely get out of bed. I hear Robin's voice in a crashing wave or the wind in some seaside pine. She's in the hum of our old TV set in the den.

Sometimes, when I'm in the checkout line at the Red and White, it's as if she just popped back in for another box of Smarties. She always did that. And then someone will tell me they're ever so sorry for my loss, and I'm pulled right back into the nightmare my life has become since she died.

I've attached another photo taken a year or two after the last one. That blue plastic bucket she's holding there? She built a thousand sandcastles with that. In fact, she used it just last summer to collect seashells. She'd gathered an exquisite mass of periwinkles, mussels, clams, and sand dollars, and had gone back to the car for a towel to haul away even more when an errant wave wrenched the whole thing out to sea. Sand pail and all.

Another rogue wave, it seems, has ripped her own gentle self from me now, body and soul. I can hardly bear it.

Tilda Campion

❀

From: Slogan@supernet.com
To: Tcampion@supernet.com
Subject: Robin

Dear Mrs. Campion,
As you probably know, Shanty is off with Biff's outfit on the logging harvest over by White Bay. He'll be gone till at least the middle of September.

I don't usually look on his computer, but he's been so low lately what with Robin and all, that I thought I'd have a quick shifty and so I ran across your e-mails. Robin was my best friend in all the world, and I know it's far worse you being her mom, but everyone is crushed from losing her.

My brother never wanted you to know, but for his sake, I have to tell you the truth about that night.

Shanty's told you about going to see Harry Martin in Corner Brook, but that's just the half of it. Mr. Martin was playing, but Shanty didn't take us down. Robin and I went with Blaine Jernigan, a senior at Central. He'd told us about some party near the docks, and I talked Robin into going with me.

Parents don't like to see these things. I know my mom didn't. But Blaine does a lot of meth. If you want a hit, he's your go-to guy. Me and Robin got into that about a year ago. At least I did. Robin started up just a few months ago. Anyway, Shanty got wind of things, as big brothers sometimes do, and he drove down to get us.

We started for home around midnight, just like he says. That's a pretty lonely stretch of road, and Shanty knows better than to speed when there's moose around. He was at the wheel and Robin was in the front seat. But she wouldn't keep her seat belt on, and round about where the 430 goes up north there by Deer Lake, she started opening her door and slamming it shut over and over again.

Shanty was afraid she meant to jump out, so he reached across to pull her back. But she just kept laughing and laughing and slapping at him. He must have lost control of the car before we could stop. I don't remember what happened after that. Just that the roadside marsh got closer and closer in slow motion.

And then I must have blacked out.

Shanty said you'd suffered enough having lost your only child. So he asked me not to tell anyone. About Robin or the meth. No mom wants to hear her baby girl is a meth head. But Constable Harcourt can tell you the whole truth. Maybe that's why you've never asked him for details and he was hesitant to give them.

Shanty's the best big brother anybody could have, Mrs. Campion. He's been like a dad to me since our own left when I was about five. But sometimes his heart is just too big for his own good. So, I'm begging you, Mrs. Campion, don't do this to him. No more pictures. No more guilt. He doesn't deserve it.

Carla Logan

From: Tcampion@supernet.com
To: Slogan@supernet.com
Subject: Robin

Dear Carla,

I know Shanty's still over by White Bay, so I hope you'll be reading this in his stead and can pass it on. It's been a lengthy, strange, and very difficult struggle to come to terms with your last letter, which is why I've waited so long to answer. I did indeed check with Constable Harcourt, and to my everlasting devastation and heartbreak, he confirmed all that you said.

I am shattered. Absolutely gutted. I no longer have reason to doubt your brother's motives or actions, and so I can only fall back on the good man you say he is. Please convey to him my deepest apologies and let him know, if you can, that the forgiveness he thought he needed from me, I now ask of him.

Best,
Tilda Campion

From: recohen@supernet.com
To: Tcampion@supernet.com
Subject: Robin

Dear Tilda,

Having missed you of late, I am deeply concerned for your welfare. Moreover, numerous phone messages I have left you have thus far gone unanswered, as have those of your many friends and acquaintances in the congregation. Nor have you answered your doorbell. You are in shock. I do understand and appreciate that. But please allow me, as your pastor, to be of some comfort and support at this very difficult time, when Robin's passing is still so raw and unbearable.

We do not always see the workings of Divinity in our lives, in the many strange coincidences or seemingly inexplicable tragedies that so often befall us. We can only turn our own lives and the lives of our loved ones over to a Higher Power and trust that there is some pattern, some divine reasoning that may, in time, comfort our souls and give us peace.

The loss of a child is particularly odious and debilitating, and we must all strive prayerfully to accept

Divine Will, even in the direst of circumstances. Regrets are inevitable even in a life well lived.

We are none so pure that we can escape the sting of remorse, or of things better left unsaid. But a burden of guilt serves only to nullify and oppress the life-spirit of we who must soldier on.

So it is now with Shanty's death in White Bay.

We may never have all the answers. A "logging accident" seems overly simplistic and painfully nonspecific. It gives us no solace, no measure of discernment or acceptance, more especially if we look to the past instead of struggling to face the future. So I must tell you again that you do not have to bear your burden alone.

Sincerely,
Reverend Cohen

Loti

*(A Three-Stranded Yellow
Polyester Rope)*

*Common Birdsfoot Trefoil—**Loti** Corniculati—an abundant and sprawling species, belongs to the pea family. Its vibrant yellow flowers, sometimes streaked with red and bunched in small clusters at the end of a short stem, resemble tiny slippers. Its pods look like claws or birds' feet. Macerated, this variety of trefoil releases small quantities of cyanide.*

SO HERE THEY SIT, Loti and Quinn, seaside in downtown Miami. He wants to talk about Sharnique's birthday. She wants to throw her drink in his face.

Through the frizzed tangle of her short, strawberry-blond hair, Loti is watching a line of cruise ships stacked across the water by South Beach like the city blocks of a small town. She's been waitressing at Bobbi Crump's Seafood Emporium in the Bayside Marketplace, which is where they are now, having lunch outside under the palm trees, picking their way through blackened grouper and shrimp. (Half-priced for employees.)

It's clouding over and the breeze has dulled, but it's still humid. The air hums with the rattle and rhythms of down-town Miami—salsa bands, loud and incessant Spanish ac-cents, the rush and roar of city traffic, the staccato of Cuban-American dancers on the boardwalk. Big hair, bright colors, short skirts.

Quinn is living with Janelle now, another Bobbi Crump waitress . . . and Loti's former best friend. She took to his straw hats, blousy shirts, and troubadour personality like ice to whiskey. Loti likes to think she hates them both equally, but Janelle, who's probably never weighed an ounce over a hundred pounds in her twenty-one years, and whose thick auburn hair never frizzes in Florida's damp heat, actually comes in a distant second. Loti itches to see Quinn eradi-cated from their daughter's life like the cockroach he is.

Two massive bridges span the deep army-green seawater of Biscayne Bay. Drawing from Loti's vacant gaze behind her black sunglasses, Quinn knows the water is lapping thickly at the pier, garbage littering its inner edges. And all the way over to the towering hotel line of Miami Beach, moored yachts and touring boats bob, and sport-fishing boats advertise sailfish and shark, dolphin and swordfish. One of these days, Quinn thinks, he's going to quit his low-pay Crump short-order cook gig, buy one of those rigs, and go to sea; make a real living for his daughter. Maybe next summer.

"Of course you can see her on her birthday," Loti says. "She's only four once. And like it or not, you *are* her father."

(*That's one year and three months I'll never get back,* Loti silently fumes. *Should have stayed in school.*)

"How would I know?" Quinn says, immediately wishing he hadn't.

Loti sighs and looks off to sea again. "Well, it's trash in the dustbin now anyway," she says. "And besides, you're the one who took up with that skinny strumpet."

She allows herself the merest glimpse of Quinn's face from the corner of her eye. "But we're here for Sharnique. She's with Ma now. I'm on till midnight."

"Ma's set the party for this Saturday, three to five, something like that," Loti tells Quinn. "Invited a bunch of snotty little brats from around the neighborhood. Saturday's the only time she could manage."

(*I checked your schedule, you prick. You're on all day. Ten to six.*)

"I'll work it out," Quinn says. Pushing back his chair as he stands, he drops a handful of coins on the tabletop. "I know you'd sooner see me dumped for gator feed than show my face," he says. And then he smiles—a flash of perfect white teeth in a sun-bronzed face—and swipes his Panama fedora from the back of his chair.

Loti has nothing more to say. With a heavy sigh, she watches Quinn walk away.

❀

LOTI CONCEDES THAT SHARNIQUE adores the shiny yellow jump rope her daddy gives her for her fourth birthday. As sleek and slippery as Quinn himself, it's a beauty, and Sharnique, whose tiny feet can barely leave the ground, spends the afternoon enthralled by her father's charm. Loti's the one who'll have to manage the baby tantrums when it's all over. She hates Quinn for that too.

Loti herself never got a skipping rope for her birthday. Instead, her daddy left the same day she turned four. Loti doesn't remember much about him other than his name.

Hector.

And Hector had a mean streak. Emptied the waste bin on the kitchen floor once, yelling something about money being kept from him. Or maybe it was whiskey. After he'd moved out, Loti's ma groused about Hector all the time. She always backed a rant with a bucket of tears. Loti never knew if they were real or not. It was all a bit confusing.

In the end, Loti and her ma lived all cramped up in a one-bedroom flat in Overtown. When Quinn left, Loti had to go back there with Sharnique and drown in the whirlpool of her mother's bitterness. She hates Quinn for that too.

❧

THE HARBOR TOUR BOAT *Sea Gypsy* leaves the Bayside Marketplace dock just short of eleven in the morning, in the care of Frederico, captain and tour guide. A long, bowed bridge leads out of downtown Miami to the fringe of trees that marks Virginia Key, the first of the Florida Keys. And then the heaped containers, monster cranes, and offshore rusted pontoon-dredgers of Miami's commercial seaport come into view, the *Seabound Intrepid* from Panama among the freighters at anchor.

"Quinn's not a bad lad, Loti," her mother says. "Cost him half a week's wages, this." She waves her free hand vaguely out over the open water, holding Sharnique's hand with the other.

"He plays you, Ma. Always did. You've never been on a harbor cruise your whole life."

"This is a fine and generous thing he's given Sharnique for her birthday, Loti. For all of us. Brought her that fancy jump rope too."

Loti fingers the smooth nylon rope inside her shoulder bag. It's a beauty, alright. Three strands of twisted yellow plastic and polyester rope, with green foam handles. And a stopwatch.

"She's a baby, Ma. What's a baby gonna do with a stop-watch?"

(*What the hell is a baby supposed to do with a stop-watch?*)

"It's the thought of it, Loti. It's the thought of it. Sharnique's not much of a baby anymore anyway, is she?"

"We'll see," Loti says. "We'll see."

They cruise past Fisher Island, bristling with celebrity mansions and private yachts. And then comes Star Island, a sun-bleached paradise of balconied great houses with massive swimming pools, turrets, gardens, guesthouses, wide green lawns, and palm trees.

Loti's ma, who prefers the boat's enclosed seating, goes inside, and Sharnique is on the lookout for a dolphin or a manatee, neither of which, Loti knows, could thrive in such fuel-laden water. Chugging back into port, the *Sea Gypsy* passes a troop of brown pelicans, each posed atop a stunted pier pylon. And these Sharnique names, one by one, as they pass them by. Named and numbered, they're soon far behind, and Sharnique slips inside to finish the day in her grandmother's lap.

Alone on the deck, Loti stares down as empty beer cans and soda bottles eddy with coconut shells and masses of matted grass. Sharnique will never know when Loti pulls up her daddy's yellow skipping rope and hurls it over the guardrail.

Red

(A Disposable Syringe)

Red Clover—Trifolium pratense—has been naturalized in many parts of the world. Its dark, short-lived pink flowers form a dense inflorescence. Excessive ingestion of Red Clover may cause infertility.

I DIDN'T KNOW HER at all. I only stayed at her Prince Edward Island B&B—Keelan's Holiday Farm—a couple of days last summer. Completely by chance. I guess her husband called her Red because of that wild mane of auburn hair. I thought it was her name until just now. Reading the newspaper, I see that her given name was Skyler.

I WAS DOWN EAST then, on a self-guided tour of Maritime Canada. There's a roundabout in Pictou where the road goes out to the Prince Edward Island ferry out of Caribou. The Northumberland Ferries Limited's *Confederation*. The run is about seventy-five minutes.

It was a bright blue day in early July.

The ferry is compact and there were no waves to speak of in the Northumberland Strait, so it was an easy ride. PEI soon came in sight, a long, low streak of land on the horizon.

We reached the dock at Wood Island, and I motored across the province to Cavendish, where I had reservations at a B&B on the North Shore called Clear Waters Inn.

PEI is a treasure trove of brilliantly green pastures, grassy hills, and fields dotted with cylinders of cut hay. And all of it bounded by thick summer trees—maples, oaks, and beeches—and tidy farmsteads with gable-roofed wooden homes. The soil is iron red, and cormorants gathered on all the causeways and bridges en route. Having come from wild Cape Breton's empty seastrands and high fir forests, PEI felt safe and secure.

My cottage at Clear Waters was a one-room pine and plasterboard affair with walls as thin as paper. Kids swarmed everywhere, hollering to one another, and beach towels clung to every railing.

That area by Cavendish is a mecca for domesticated tourism. Waterslides, miniature golf, and, of course, the beach.

I left my luggage in my appointed room and went out for a lobster supper at New Glasgow, five or six miles down the road, a commendable meal served with mussels, fish chowder, and crusty homemade rolls. The next morning, I prowled the cemetery where the Maritime writer Lucy Maud Montgomery is buried—in a much-flowered granite tomb embellished with ivy. An interesting woman, Lucy. She called her part of the island "the haunt of ancient peace." And tight with the spirits of the island, she was said to talk to the trees. I liked her more for that.

Afterward, I went up to Green Gables itself, a typical island farmhouse from the 1890s, homey and quaint, all the rooms filled with a rustic simplicity. Emerald meadows, deep hollows, and dark woods flowed all around the perimeter. It all felt so peaceful.

I drove up to Malpeque near the French River for deep-fried oysters at the Ocean View Restaurant in Darnley. PEI in a nutshell unfolded outside the window—pastoral fields, clouds like scoops of vanilla ice cream.

But back to Red.

The very next night, Saturday, I stayed at Keelan's Holiday Farm, the B&B she ran with her husband—Keelan—just outside of North Rustico.

Red's people were among the earliest settlers on the North Shore, and this was their family homestead. The farmhouse was built in 1816 and seemed upheaved and overly cluttered, though the surroundings were sublime. Gentle hills of long summer grass and mauve lupins, with a straight-on view of the sea. I'd reached Keelan's after taking in a couple of secluded cemeteries in the empty countryside nearby.

After settling in my room, I came down for tea in Red's kitchen. Keelan, a boisterous, gregarious young man of the hunter/fisher sort, talked his way through a tattered photo album, spinning yarns of moose racks, deer points and coyote kills, and fishing excursions in remote Avalon ponds. As Red set about laying on supper, Keelan vanished downstairs, and I could hear him pounding on the piano, backed by the squeals of their three older children, all under the age of six. The baby, Austin, sat at Red's feet, beside the stove, bashing the stained linoleum with a wooden spoon.

I was the only guest that night, though from the chaos at the table, Red might have been feeding a small army. All the children fidgeted and squirmed, each demanding their mother's undivided attention. Keelan sat bouncing the baby on his knee, oblivious to the turmoil.

In the morning, Austin woke up at four forty-three. I know this because I looked at my backlit watch. He then bawled continuously for two solid hours. At seven o'clock, I finally heard Keelan's voice, loud and rankled. "Red?" he called. "What's the matter, dear? Red?"

He'd done the same over the course of the previous evening, adding repeatedly, "What is going on here?" Only rarely had Red responded. From the safety of my upstairs room, I saw him step outside for a smoke, while Red cleared the table, reordered her kitchen, and readied each child for bed. By 8:00 p.m., the kids had been running wild for hours, and Red was fit to be locked up.

I was off sightseeing most of the next day, but on that last night, Sunday, poor Red had it bad. She tallied up for Keelan every strained effort she'd made to keep the kids in line. And then she threw on her sweater and said she was going out for a walk. Keelan just smiled and went on telling me about pike and bull moose and ice fishing on Malpeque Bay at the winter solstice. I remember thinking at the time that it would all make a pretty compelling story.

I left Monday morning in a thick white fog as Keelan headed off on foot to put in his time at the fish market on Harbourview Drive.

Somehow I feel I should have known, but I never dreamed she'd take that battered old green Chevy parked out front and drive it off the North Rustico pier. And with all those little kids inside. From the puncture marks on their bodies, she must have sedated them first with something they haven't yet identified.

I have to say, I never saw that coming.

Mari

(A Plastic Cigarette Lighter)

*Many parts of the showy Marsh **Mari**gold–Caltha palus-*
tris–are mildly poisonous with an irritant that can cause
skin rashes. With its broad heart-shaped leaves, Marsh
Marigold is one of the most imposing plants of the
machair.

MIRRORS WEREN'T PARTICULARLY kind to Mari anymore. Her eyelids puffed and her cheekbones went flat. But she still had the most exquisite eyes, a cross between clear pale "ginger-jade"—as the press used to call it—and translucent emerald. Those eyes were the single virtue to be gleaned from the *New York Times* review. Mari scanned the headline again: *Mari Goldman's Comeback Quietly Impressive; The Eyes Still Have It.*

At the top of the column, upper left-hand, was a black-and-white photo of a big-eyed girl with short spiky hair who looked all of thirteen.

"Trollop." Mari sniffed and tossed the newspaper aside. How could anyone that young possibly appreciate theater and performance? And where exactly had Mari Goldman gone, pray tell? She'd been working steadily now for a hundred years or more, some of those rather lean.

Pivoting back to the mirror, she pulled an ivory-handled brush through her hair, no longer its signature blond. Mari had been browbeaten by the director into reverting to her natural shade, a wispy, sugary champagne.

"Mary Tyrone in Eugene O'Neill's *Long Day's Journey into Night*," he'd enthused with all the simplicity and ignorance of his thirty-nine years, "is one of the juiciest roles for mature women."

Clearly Mari Goldman was a good deal older than Mary Tyrone. But an artist of Mari's "stature, talent, and peerless reputation" should have no trouble carrying it off "au naturel." He'd lobbed that last snitty remark with a smirk that convinced Mari that he'd just flashed on her *mature* body naked in the shower.

"What can such a—*boy*—know about these things anyway?" she asked the image in the mirror as she bent to finger the profusion of age lines on her forehead. Their length and depth were disconcerting, as were the furrows that arced from the outer corners of her eyes, down across her gaunt cheekbones, to expire at the edges of her frowning lips.

Still more wrinkles etched the hollows of her cheeks, like a fine gossamer webbing. Gone were the days when men of all ages, cultures, classes, and tastes had praised that face with words like "porcelain," "perfection," and "paragon."

Mari dropped her eyes from the foreign image in the mirror and smiled, catching in her mind's eye her very first screen test. 1941. Los Angeles. First days of the war. She was five years old. Yet as young as she was, she'd been spellbound by the imagination and possibility of motion pictures.

Hitchcock had been making movies since the early twenties. She'd been keen on him at once, a round bubbling man appreciative of her mature intellect and unrestrained precociousness. One glorious conquest followed another after that. For both of them. Mari Goldman, superstar. And after a time, only Mari. Heady days that culminated in *Eleanor*, her rave-reviewed take on Eleanor of Aquitaine. Her very own *Cleopatra*, she'd thought then—privately, of course—and for decades afterward. Liz herself could never have carried it off with half the panache and aplomb of Mari Goldman.

But that was then. And this—this closet-sized dressing room in an off-off-Broadway theater—was now. The disheveled jumble of the room behind mocked her in the dressing table mirror. Whitewashed walls had turned seedy with dust. And someone had draped a shocking-pink feather boa over the teakwood room divider collapsed against the back wall. She might as well have been playing Vegas.

She lobbed the hairbrush onto the adjacent leather divan, rooted around in her handbag, and drew up a battered packet of cigarettes and an apple-red plastic lighter. Reclining in her swivel chair, she lit up. One long, deep drag filled her lungs with smoke, which she dispensed in a feathery line toward the ceiling.

"Miss Mari."

An effeminate male voice shattered Mari's reveries, and there was a tap at the door.

"What is it, Julian?"

"There's a reporter out here from some rag in the Village. Wants a word or two before you leave?"

"Give me a minute, Jay. I'm coming."

Mari doused the cigarette in an overloaded ashtray and spritzed her tongue with mouthwash.

"No—wait." A nebulous panic boiled up in her chest. "Can you help me with my hair?"

"Of course I can, Miss Mari."

The door burst open, and a lanky young man in sequined black jeans launched himself into the room. His designer T-shirt was emblazoned with *Babes Are Toyland.*

"It's always my greatest pleasure to bring out the very

best in that glorious face," he gushed. "And if I may say so, honey, your performance tonight was dead brilliant."

"Oh, now, Jay, let's not overdo."

Julian expertly dispatched a bin of rouges, lipsticks, mascara, eye shadow, and concealer to the center of Miss Mari's dressing table. The mound threatened to bury the silver-plated cigarette lighter she'd enshrined there—a relic engraved with a curlicued *To Mari, Love Alfred*—and she tucked it surreptitiously out of the way.

"I mean every word of it," Julian said. "I'm your biggest fan, you know. Your Mary Tyrone was superb. A one-off. A tour de force. When you materialized at the top of that staircase . . ."—here Julian touched his fingers to his lips and blew a kiss to the mirror—"perfection." He leaned in, a packet of blue-green eye shadow poised next to Mari's right ear, and studied her reflection. "Well . . . that gorgeous hair just flows. I swear I was pulled right into the Tyrone drawing room, grasping at that poor woman's pain and sorrow."

Julian swayed forward once again, snatching up an assortment of eyeliners from the table, holding them to the light, and dropping all but one. With a flick of his wrist, he twirled Mari away from the mirror. Quick and deft strokes meticulously rendered her makeup anew.

"Your interpretation was spot-on, honey," he said as he spun Mari back into place to finish his work. "Honest to God, it was. You were brilliant, my dear."

"Well, thank you, Jay. I appreciate the rave."

Mari flinched as Julian zeroed in on her left eye with a mascara wand.

"Truth be told, I don't think I can face *any* press tonight," she said.

Julian swiped the hairbrush from the divan and stabbed it in the direction of the door. "You'll be fine," he said. "Old Branson's outside, as always. He'll see you through."

Julian drew the brush the length of Mari's hair with great gusto and swept the pile into bouffant splendor at the crown of her head.

"You. Are. Gorgeous, honey," he gushed. "Would I lie? Look at those cheekbones."

Mari cast a doubtful glance Jay's way and let her eyes drop to the mirror again. Not bad, she thought, for an ancient. Who was that actress who prattled on about looking younger by not wearing her glasses?

"Your talent knows no bounds, Jay," she said.

And she meant it.

"Oh—" Julian jabbed Mari's shoulder and grinned. His left hand lightly brushing his shoulder, his elbow resting on the back of his right hand, he contemplated her face in the mirror and resumed a precise plucking of Mari's hair so that in the end, her now radiant face was framed in wispy tendrils.

"You look like a goddess," he said. "Honest to God, girl. A Greek goddess. You'll knock 'em dead."

Mari squinted as she rose from the dressing table.

"Better them than me."

"It's raining again," Julian said, fussing with the satin folds at the waistline of Mari's pea-green gown. He adjusted the pleats in the bodice and then lunged for a dusty-blue London Fog raincoat flung across the back of the divan.

Snatching the newspaper she'd been reading, Mari stuffed it in her voluminous handbag, along with the cigarettes and red plastic lighter. She took one deep breath before Julian ushered her into the hallway to join Branson.

Tucker Branson had been Mari's New York chauffeur since before the dawn of time, it seemed, fully thirty-five years, beginning just after Branson turned eighteen. Starstruck, he'd run off to Broadway just as other adventurers might have joined the circus. Lacking any serious acting chops, he'd snapped up the opportunity to work for the incomparable Mari Goldman.

With deep affection and barefaced admiration, Mari watched him charm the young Asian-American reporter from Julian's "Village rag." Regal and impervious, he'd decked himself out in a natty three-piece suit with an off-white satin cummerbund. He towered above the tiny girl with straight slick hair the color of charcoal. Both of them glanced up as the dressing-room door opened and Mari glided through, Julian in her shadow.

"Miss Mari," the girl began. "Lulu Chong from *East Side Times*. A word or two?"

Jet-black eyes danced in a face as smooth as a rose petal.

"It's been a long night," Branson answered, taking Mari's elbow.

"How does it feel to be in the limelight again?"

"Mari Goldman has always been in the limelight."

Mari patted Branson's rough hand. "Could you bring the car around, Branson? I *am* feeling the chill tonight."

She bent toward the young girl and rested her palm lightly on Lulu's sleeveless upper arm.

"I'm not entirely up to an interview at this late hour, Miss Chong," she said. "But I would be so pleased to see you before matinee tomorrow to answer any and all questions. I'm flattered by your kind attention."

"My pleasure, Miss Goldman," Lulu answered. "One o'clock then?"

"I look forward to it."

Mari passed Lulu an effusive smile, and the girl retreated on the heels of Branson, who, donning his own rain gear, had only just now allowed himself to reach the backstage door. In another lifetime, frenzied adoration would have unfurled behind that door, but Mari sensed an emptiness there tonight, as bleak as this late September.

Julian kissed her cheek to cheek, bundled her in the blue raincoat, and maneuvered her through the door, thrusting a matching blue umbrella into Branson's hand.

It was raining again, as Julian had said—gray among the treetops and soggy underfoot. Thunder muttered above the hiss of traffic, and lightning flashes melted into washed-out city streets.

Mari waved to Julian, who stood in the rain like a sodden mother hen, and then nestled into the plush beige leather of the limo's back seat as Branson pulled away. Eighth Avenue to Central Park West, headed for Mari's elegant but hushed suite in the Drake Hotel.

The city's ceiling glowed far above them, row on row of lighted windows mounting ever upward and out of sight. Incessant rain pelted the limo's darkened windows until the lights, diffused and blurred, appeared as through tears.

"Branson," Mari said as they approached Central Park. "I know it's late, but let's go downtown to Battery Park. A glimpse of Lady Liberty would do me good, I think."

Branson eased his way through the evening's marginally lessening traffic and set off toward the Hudson River. They traveled the bleary night in silence, Mari staring absentmindedly out the window, regurgitating that awful *Times* headline.

Mari Goldman's Comeback.

Quietly Impressive.

Since when had anything Mari Goldman done been quiet? she thought, her words hinged on the edge of bitterness.

Dear Julian, bless him, had overstated himself with customary zeal, and Branson—well, Branson was her dark age knight in shining armor, always coming to her defense. Still, their protestations had been just so much overblown hyperbole.

Well. Never mind.

Outside Mari's window the rain weakened and the city glistened anew, reflected in a glitter of rain pools. Just short of 1:00 a.m., she glimpsed the dripping greenery of a nearly empty Battery Park. She broke the ride's silence with a lingering sigh, as her knight in shining armor swung into the parking lot. Mari hitched up the collar of her raincoat. Then Branson climbed out, opened the rear door, and took Mari's umbrella as he helped her out.

In the lightly wooded park, the night's darkness deepened, a clammy dampness punctured only by a line of tall lantern lights along the river walk. Other smaller lamps traced inner pathways that meandered through once blazing summer gardens.

Rivulets of rainwater from fall-tinged trees slid under Mari's collar as Branson raised the umbrella over her head and took her arm. And then, in another deep silence, they drifted from metal bench to metal bench until, nearly at the waterfront, Mari patted Branson's hand and together they sat down.

Out on Liberty Island, across the breathing bay, the burnished monument rose up in watery amber light, reaching a torch-laden arm upward in hopefulness.

"I'll just be a moment or two," Mari said after a time. "Lady Liberty always cheers me up."

Alone, she crossed over to the river's edge where she slumped against the metal barricade and listened as the water below rippled gently, shallow-blackened troughs melting into gentle arcs of light-reflected molten gold.

Mari had just begun to reminisce again when a shadowed couple emerged from the rising mist, heading her way. A man and a woman. Too late to avoid eye contact, she tugged the ample hood of her raincoat over her head and smiled weakly.

"A bit of a rough night," the woman said.

Wearing a dark fleece sweat suit, she had to be Mari's age or more, a plump and round-faced woman with short silver-gray hair.

A young man steadied her with one arm, a monstrous black opened umbrella held in the other.

A fine-looking reedy fellow, Mari thought. *Probably in his mid-twenties.*

Indeed, she answered faintly.

Through the gloom, the woman peered at Mari's shadowed face.

"Haven't I seen you somewhere before?" she asked.

Before Mari could answer, the young man's brow crinkled.

"I reckon Loreena Metzger knows ninety percent of Tyler, Texas. But this here's New York City," he said, speaking at once to both women. "I reckon you're out of your league here, Grams. Beg pardon, ma'am."

The man's gentle smile told Mari he was well accustomed to impetuous behavior from his grandmother.

"Not a problem," she replied. "Though I doubt we've met before. I've never been to Tyler, Texas, myself. At least not that I remember." She laughed.

"Oh, no—no—not from back home." Loreena persisted. She shook her head and looked thoughtfully at the inky water swirling below them.

"Wait—wait," she said. "It'll come to me. I never forget a face."

"We'd best mosey on back to the hotel, Grams," the young man suggested. "Matinee tomorrow, remember?"

"Bucket list," he said to Mari with a laugh. "First Broadway show. First time in New York City."

"That's it!" Loreena exclaimed. "The matinee tomorrow reminded me. Oh—you know, Chauncey. Who's that actress from *Eleanor*?"

Mari's ears prickled. She drew in a slow, deep breath. But Chauncey only glanced at her and shrugged.

"Her picture was in the paper. Just yesterday. You must know."

Loreena swung back to Mari.

"You look exactly like Mari Goldman. Yes. Mari Goldman. That's her," she told Chauncey. "She looks just like her."

"I'm sorry to say that I'm not at all familiar with the name," Mari lied.

Here it comes, she thought. *The "quietly impressive" has-been. What's to notice beyond ginger-jade eyes?*

"She was a glory in that film," Loreena enthused.

Mari's heart skipped.

"Anybody with an achievement like that in their back pocket, well, what does it matter what's said about her now? She was a glory in that film, I'm telling you. A glory. And glory like that *never* fades."

In her peripheral vision, Mari saw the gallant Branson rise to come to her rescue, and she motioned him back with a discreet wave of her hand.

"This is a fine, fine city, Grams," Chauncey said.

Loreena's eyes fluttered from the glowing statue in the bay, to the glitter of high-rises behind her, and then came to rest on Mari's shadowed face.

"You take care, now," she said, and squeezed Mari's forearm.

Chauncey slipped a gentle, guiding hand in the crook of his grandmother's arm, and the pair of them drifted off into the night.

For a fleeting moment, Mari stared out at the monument glowing across the heaving bay and then pulled the newspaper and the apple-red cigarette lighter from her handbag. And just as Branson arrived, she lit the one with the other and tossed them both into the bay.

Scilla

(A Wine Bottle Cork)

*Common Bluebell, once known as **Scilla** non-scripta,
roots deep into coastal soils to generate a long, nodding,
one-sided row of sweet-scented violet-blue tubular
flowers.*

BY THE TIME SHE saw Joujou, Scilla had all but settled on a
nunnery. How handy then to have read about Quebec City's
Ursuline Convent on her flight. All seventeenth-century
arched windows in small casements, massive brick chim-
neys, and sharply slanted medieval rooflines.

As for Scilla and Brodie, they'd actually come undone
years ago. Their off-chance meeting at a Chicago Bar Association function had been more about opportunity and flirtation than anything else. Scilla, barely twenty years old at
the time, and a lowly prelaw student with dreams of her
own practice, had swiftly moved into an internship in
Brodie's office and then, as if by magic, into Brodie's bed.

Marriage soon followed and even now, ten years down
the road, Scilla couldn't quite recall exactly how all of that
had happened. The marriage itself still felt like someone

else's idea, a spontaneity that once set in motion had been impossible to stop. But the stars had never really aligned for them, and love, if it had ever been in the mix at all, had been quickly and quietly subsumed by corporate duty and proper appearance.

Brodie, nearly fifteen years Scilla's senior, was gone now, barely two months after her divorce papers had been served—a massive heart attack capping off his opening statement in a high-profile murder trial.

Her timing could have been better, Scilla conceded. And where else might she have been impetuous and self-serving? Yet she'd never actively wished Brodie any ill will. How better to honor his life than to make something more of her own?

And then, just as she'd allowed herself to reach that conclusion, mentally calculating the possibility of law school, her older sister, Veronica, had seemed to whisper, "Old Scilla, the Sea Monster," in her ear—as she'd done a thousand times before—most recently on the phone that morning as Scilla set off for the airport.

Perhaps hospice work would be more appropriate after all.

Veronica had had a thing for Brodie, dating back to the moment she'd first laid lustful eyes on him. And frankly, Scilla had thought more than once over the years about retreating from her particular field of marital battle and leaving Veronica the spoils. Especially following some particularly odious evening of corporate entertaining.

When Scilla's plane banked eastward, she glanced back as the coldly white winter sun slipped behind the glitter of lights running up and down Chicago's shoreline. Very soon after that, she watched as the farm fields of Michigan, plowed and flattened, stretched out below, dusted with snow like thin slats of painted wood.

In actual fact, Scilla had been named for her once

feisty, long-deceased maternal grandmother, Priscilla. But ever since she'd immersed herself in Greek mythology in the early years of high school, Veronica had taken to likening her baby sister to the Aegean sea monster Scylla, who'd so enlivened Aeneas's travels in *The Aeneid*.

Scylla inhabited a sea cave to one side of the narrow maritime passage thought by many to lie between Sicily and the Italian coast. She demanded a sacrifice of six able-bodied crewmen from any passing ship. At the other side of the channel, the mighty whirlpool Charybdis threatened to suction away any ship that happened past.

Over the years, in rivaled sisterly fashion, Veronica had mercilessly considered Scilla's many love interests in terms of Scylla's lecherous demands. How could Brodie possibly have escaped being yet another? Veronica had asked. Rhetorically, of course, but with great distain.

And then there was Scilla's mother, Helena, fabled in her own right. A woman of strident and unwavering conservative opinion, Helena, too, had condemned Scilla's perceived trouncing of Brodie's memory. A woman's duty, she said. A man's need, she said. The sanctity of marriage. And so on, and so on. And when Scilla had announced her intention of making good on Brodie's New Year's reservations at the Fairmont Château Frontenac in Quebec City, well . . . was that really wise? How would that look? What would people think?

"Oh, you know Brodie, Mother," Scilla had countered. "Wouldn't he have wanted things to go on as ever?"

She had said this not knowing, even then, if it had been true.

"You can't expect a man of Brodie's intellect and energy to be off gathering flowers day after day, conjuring up magical moments and whatnot," Helena had continued, however disjointed the thought.

If there had ever been any magic in Scilla and Brodie's relationship, it had long vanished. And yet in some small way, her mother might be right. Could Scilla have been too selfish, less empathetic, more needy, not smart enough, not strong enough, too controlling? And then back she'd go, straight into the convent again.

❦

A FIRST-TIME VISITOR, Scilla had considered her short, restricted view of Montreal as dull and unimpressive, and she moved through the terminal crowd methodically, a lengthy subterranean trek bringing her to the proper gate for her Quebec City connection.

Close to eight o'clock, they'd boarded.

The ensuing flight proved quite pretty, well below the cloud ceiling, with strings of lights meandering between the scattered towns and villages below, much of the ground bluish white with snow in the gathering darkness.

Quebec City had been nearly fogbound when they landed, but Scilla's taxi brought her through the ancient outer walls of the old city, through narrow streets aglow with Christmas décor, to deposit her in the twinkling courtyard of the fairy tale that was the stately turreted Château.

And now, she'd thoroughly steeped herself in Old Quebec. She'd even taken in the Ursuline Convent. Hadn't signed up as yet, but the museum there, both educational and compelling, was sheer delight, filled with paintings and sculptures and textiles.

At the Palais Montcalm in Place D'Youville, each footfall on the outer steps had produced a different color, another musical note. She'd dined on French onion soup and sugar pie in the cozy Saint Alexandre Pub and taken the chill off with a hot Caribou cocktail of red wine, whiskey, and maple syrup.

Off Rue Champlain, in the dark, she'd climbed the

wooden staircase up Cap Diamant to Battlefields Park, where empty rolling hills, white with freshly fallen snow, were tracked with ski ruts and snowboard furrows, the odd bared winter tree silhouetted against the night's pale sky. Below, the black St. Lawrence rolled by silently, beyond cobblestone streets of Old Town that glowed like old Victorian Christmas cards.

The ten-minute ferry, *Alphonse Desjardins*, had conveyed her across the river to Lévis, ice floes speeding past to the soothing recorded sound of some Québécois balladeer. The ice had frozen in layers like sheets of mica, so that the edges broke in artful geometric patterns, and as ferries plied their way back and forth, these had coalesced in long, jagged ridges.

On deck just briefly, bundled up against the searing cold, she'd admired the city anew as the Château rose up grandly above the lower town, backed by the hazy, distant heights of the Laurentians. On retreat, she'd lost her footing and deposited the bottle of Domaine de Lavoie 2015 she'd picked up in Lévis on a passing block of ice. The wine diffused in vibrant cerise, the cork upright at the center like the eye of a wild rose.

Sunday morning, after she'd stuffed herself at the Château's justly famous brunch buffet—shrimp in the shell and salmon mousse; caribou stew and beef Wellington; camembert and crêpes suzette; pâtés, eggs Benedict, croque-en-bouche, petits fours, and tartlets—all the confusion and guilt she'd kept at bay with such distractions had very nearly brought her to tears.

At that very moment then, her server, the vivacious Monique, had brought Joujou to her attention. Monique's twin brother, Jean-Phillippe—budding magician Monsieur Joujou—was working down in the old town at the Maison de la Chanson.

❧

SO IT WAS THAT Scilla found herself on Rue du Petit-Champlain in old Quebec City on New Year's Eve. Shop fronts, in buildings that dated back centuries, lined the street, their interiors blazing with a cozy, inviting warmth. The Quartier had been a merchant area for over four hundred years, Monique had told her.

Tiny white Christmas lights outlined windows and doorways, and overhead, blue electric light bulbs accented with illuminated snowflakes dipped across the street in festive garlands. Nearly every store front had a Christmas tree standing on the front stoop, on a doorstep, or on a staircase, the street itself a radiant stretch of high-slung wall sconces, candlelit lantern posts, and fluttering red velvet Christmas ribbon. Everywhere, a gentle snowfall dusted footpaths and alleyways.

A magical part of town, Scilla thought, as she stepped out of the cold into the warmth of Maison de la Chanson. Les Petits Chanteurs de Charlesbourg had just wrapped up their performance, an offering of primarily French-Canadian Christmas carols, as Scilla noted from the open program a rather breathless greeter thrust into her hand.

"*Bienvenue! Bienvenue!*" the elderly woman enthused. "And welcome, most welcome you are, madame. Monsieur Joujou begins soon now."

With an exaggerated flourish of her free hand, the old woman directed Scilla to a small table tucked into a corner at the rear of the room.

"Sit now, there in the front, my good lady." She patted the back of Scilla's gloved hand. "To the one side or the other, just as you please. But sit. Sit."

And Scilla did.

She dropped her parka, her earmuffs, her fur-lined

gloves, and her twice-wrapped alpaca scarf on the back of the lone chair to the left of Joujou's table—the one nearest the rear door.

A smattering of patrons had begun to mill about monsieur's corner table, though none of them had as yet chosen a seat, of which there were several dozen.

Scilla had just resolved to head back to the hotel when Jean-Phillippe materialized from parts unknown, a slight, handsome young man with a full head of spiky black hair and a manicured curlicue moustache. He was resplendent in immaculately pressed satin-collared coattails.

"*Bienvenue! Bienvenue!*" he shouted above the rising murmur of the crowd, sweeping his long arms left and right. "They say magic is the only honest profession. I promise to deceive you. And I will. So come! Come, *mes amis!* And oh . . . you . . . you lovely ladies."

He winked broadly as a trio of young women wended their way from the front of the hall with their escorts.

"*Et beaux hommes! Asseyez-vous!* Sit! Sit!"

And they all did, laughing amongst themselves.

"Are you alone, dear lady?" With the same glint in his eye, Joujou addressed the middle-aged woman Scilla had just watched settle into the last empty seat in the front row.

"I am indeed, monsieur," the woman answered, stashing a pair of hand-knit mittens into the front pockets of her woolen overcoat.

"Oh—then come sit here with me, *ma chérie.*" He winked broadly again and patted the chair immediately to his right, and the crowd quieted as the woman came forward.

Joujou took her hand with a gallant flourish and dipped his head conspiratorially. "And what would you be doing after the show?" he asked in a stage whisper that brought a smile even to Scilla's face.

"Then if we are to be lovers, *ma chérie*"—and the audience snickered as Joujou pulled a deck of cards from his pocket—"I must know your name."

"Jenny. Well, Jennifer, actually. But all my friends call me Jenny."

"Jenny it is, then. And so we are fast friends now, eh, Jenny?"

The woman nodded, and Joujou began a meticulous shuffling of his cards.

"I must tell you all, my friends, that magic is always and ever a misdirection," Joujou began again. "But now, my sweet Spinning Jenny, you must pick for me one card." And holding the deck up to face her, he began to smoothly run the index finger of his right hand through them. "Now look at me, Jenny," Joujou said. "*Regardez-moi, ma chérie.* Visualize that card, my Spinning Jenny. Say it in your mind." And he quickly withdrew the deck. "You have in your mind your card?" he asked.

The woman nodded.

"Now as you are as dear to my heart as life itself, I tell you that I keep your card here in my pocket." And he pulled up the three of diamonds from the left inside pocket of his jacket. "Now is this your card then, sweet Jenny?"

Jenny let out a soft gasp and nodded.

Scilla did much the same and the audience erupted in applause, some in the front rows pulling their chairs in closer.

"All the world is full of magic, my friends," Joujou said as he brought up a small handful of coins from his right pocket. "But you must always, always, I say, know it is there. Your head . . . *la tête*, eh?" He tapped his forehead. "Your head says to you, no, no, *this* is not so. Or . . . you must not believe *that*. But, *mes amis*, you say to me that you don't believe something? Does that mean it is not real?"

One by one, as he spoke, he laid four silver coins and one large copper one on the tabletop.

"Let us say you and I." He leaned forward slightly and brushed Jenny's shoulder. "We will perhaps see the sunrise together tomorrow, eh, *ma petite?*"

Scilla was certain she'd seen Jenny blush.

"*La science*, eh? The light refracts, eh? Motes of dust in the air, eh? But the morning comes and the night goes. Is not that magic? So now, can it not be that everything is magic or nothing is? We are, each one of us, surrounded by things we cannot see. How can this not create in us so great a wonder? Now can you all see these coins?"

The small crowd mumbled its agreement.

"You can all see these coins?" Joujou placed four of the five into Jenny's opened hand and closed her fingers on them. "Hold them tight, my Spinning Jenny. Four in the hand and I have one, *non?*"

He tapped Jenny's hand, and when she opened her fist, all five coins lay in her palm.

Applause. Applause.

"So, now, *ma chérie*, do *you* believe in magic?" Scilla was chagrined to find that Joujou was looking at her. "And what is your name, dear lady?"

"Scilla," she answered.

"Ah, then I am most assured that you have been called more than once in your short and beautiful life a sea monster. Is this not so?"

"Oh, yes," Scilla answered, with a roll of her eyes. "Yes, I have."

"Well, I tell you this now, *ma chérie* . . ." He took her right hand and laid it palm up on the tabletop. "Between Scylla and Charybdis, they say. This is—how do you say—between the rock and the hard place? No . . . no . . . I tell you this is not so. A sacrifice of six good men comes out of fear. Is this not so? Courage, dear Scilla. Charybdis is courage. Take courage, *ma petite*. You see what I am telling you?"

Joujou didn't wait for a reply.

"Now, *ma chérie*, I am going to drop this coin from above on the count of three, and I want you to grab it in this hand when it lands. *Comprend?*" He sat back a moment and looked out on his audience. "*Le courage*," he said. "Ah . . . *le courage* I must conjure up to come out to all of you and work like this, eh?"

The audience broke out in applause. Joujou smiled back grandly and turned back to Scilla.

"*Maintenant . . . un . . . deux . . . trois.*" And the coin appeared to drop down into Scilla's palm. She closed her fingers on it at once. But when Joujou instructed her to open her fist, the coin had vanished.

"Life is like magic, you see, my friends," he said, and plucked the same coin from behind Scilla's right ear. "In life as in magic, what matters is where we put our attention. You may say that even in death this is so. When something leaves this world, something else comes into it."

Joujou went on like this for an hour or more. He produced a rabbit from an empty top hat, a fan of cards out of thin air, a shower of coins in an empty bucket. He made coins and doves appear and then disappear again. He restored cut ropes and torn newspapers, filled soap bubbles with smoke, and blew the spots off playing cards.

Scilla took in the depth and breadth of Joujou's words, the wonder of each and every magical trick he played, and before long, she found herself completely free of Veronica's criticisms, of Helena's disappointments, and of her own ambivalence. She went on to celebrate the New Year on the Grande Allée with fireworks, optimism, and a clear conscience.

And when she got back to Chicago late the next day,

Scilla took courage and told both her mother and her sister that she understood now that neither her life nor her love had been meant for Brodie. She would mourn his passing, of course. But she was going back to law school.

Ruby

(A Green Plastic Laundry Basket)

*Salt-tolerant Sea Thrift–*Armeria maritima*–prefers water-logged soils. Carpets of low tufted clumps send up long stems topped with globes of bright pink flowers. One hybrid subspecies, Bee's* **Ruby***–Rubrifolia–produces large cherry-red blossoms.*

RUBY LAY OFFSHORE, NOT expected to make landfall until 5:00 p.m. A hint of her potential lay in the brisk breeze that had flared up overnight and in the swell of black-bottomed clouds that now darkened the eastern horizon. Such potent winds might dry just one more load of worn work-shirts before the rain. Jolene could collect them again before her shift began at Mags Diner, if time allowed.

Ruby was the second major storm to set a course for the Carolina coast that summer. Tropical Storm Andrea hit the first week in June, nearly two months ago, a backdoor storm sliding in from the Gulf of Mexico. Happily, Jolene had been at her cousin Lupita's in Wichita then.

She took a deep breath, propped her mother's green plastic wash basket on the upstairs railing, and eyed the long line of moss-draped live oaks that stretched out toward

Jeremy Creek. Like so many other buildings in McClellanville and all up and down the coast, Jolene's daddy's house pushed up grandly from a wide green lawn, built on nine-foot stilts.

Jolene gathered her chestnut hair into a loose ponytail at the nape of her neck, hoisted the battered basket to her right hip, and started down the outside staircase.

It wasn't as though Jolene hadn't suffered rough storms before. Hurricane Allison hit Charleston the year she was born. Since then, there had been no shortage of hurricanes, tropical storms, and depressions. Hannah, Irene, Earl, Charley—all of these had at least touched on McClellanville. And each of them, but for Allison, still inhabited Jolene's psyche like a bad dream. Category 1 Hurricane Irene had taken her mother's life just three years ago, the day after Jolene's sixteenth birthday.

Jolene's mother, Celeste, had survived Hugo, a legendary Category 4 hurricane, whose story Celeste had never tired of telling. The family had relocated from West Texas earlier that September, settling at Goose Creek, a tiny village about twenty miles inland from Charleston. Far enough away to ride out the storm—or so they thought. They'd boarded up, sandbagged, and huddled down.

"Aye, *la pesadilla, chiquita*," Celeste had told her daughter each time a new storm threatened. "The worst nightmare of my life."

From midnight on, after Hugo roared ashore, broken branches and uprooted trees, backyard sheds, washing machines, and even refrigerators slammed the house hour after hour. Roofing tiles, loosened lumber, plumbing fixtures, shingles, garbage, and car parts. Trees snapped like fireworks, and downed power lines sizzled in the floodwaters.

"The wind howled like an oncoming train," Celeste said. "Peeling away our home layer by layer like an onion. The roof went and we were soaked to the bone, shivering in the dark like scalded dogs. Waiting to die."

By morning, the mauled house had shifted a foot off its foundation.

"*Dios mío, chiquita!*" she always told Jolene. "I hope you are spared such a storm. Terror like that stays with you your whole life."

After Hugo relented, Celeste had pleaded with her parents to take her back to the dryness of West Texas. But her daddy had come to work cotton up on the Piedmont, and money like that was hard to come by. Celeste turned twenty that year and had just settled her own plans to make the trip in the spring. But that was before she met Jesse, Jolene's daddy, CJ, at the shrimp festival in McClellanville. She found herself pregnant soon after and the couple quickly married, only to lose the child to a miscarriage. Things should have ended right there, Jolene often thought. But Celeste had been raised to stay the course.

One by one, Jolene shook out her daddy's shirts and clipped them into place on a nylon wash line that sagged between two palmettos in the back yard.

CJ, who was known around town as Cap'n Jesse, had endured Hugo too. But he'd been born to the sea, shrimping from Jeremy Creek on the *Missy Nona*, his father's trawler, for most of his life. CJ's Hugo story, which Jolene had heard at least as often as she'd heard Celeste's, gave off the heady whiff of adventure, where her mother had only smelled fear.

Somehow, CJ had managed to be in Charleston when Hugo made landfall on Sullivan's Island. With several hundred city residents, he'd taken refuge in the Omni Hotel down by the seawall. Power outages had begun an hour earlier, with snapped electrical poles and orphaned wires dangling over flooded streets. By 1:00 p.m., the hotel's windows began to bulge, some of them popping like soda bottles.

Inside the hotel, they'd barricaded the doors. Piled sand-bags in front. And while occasional lightning bolts shot through the darkness, rain sluiced down outside like water wrung from a sponge. A twenty-foot tidal surge ripped through town, and ninety-mile-an-hour winds roared outside.

Unlike Celeste, Jesse had reveled in it all. Being on the dirty side of weather—to the northeast in the case of a Carolina hurricane—never failed to set his blood thumping.

"If a tropical depression so much as thinks of forming out in the Atlantic," he'd be saying now, wherever the *Missy Nona* had docked, "it's The Big One. We're all gonna drown, blown to smithereens like piss in the wind, when like as not, we'll be sittin' in traffic six ways to Sunday, hours from gettin' back home. And them folks that stayed put will be out grillin' on the beach."

He'd said this even after Irene pinned Celeste under a clump of palmetto fronds. She'd been cut clear, but CJ had found her next to him in bed the next morning, dead from a blood clot that had traveled to her heart from the site of the impact.

Cap'n Jesse continued to be a fair-weather father after they lost Celeste and still spent most of his time out on the *Missy Nona*. The white shrimp harvest would follow the brown, and CJ would shrimp into early January. Even in the off-season, he'd trawl ahead of harbor dredgers, rescuing loggerheads and leatherbacks. Just short of four this morning, Jolene had heard him pottering about in the kitchen. He'd have left the dock by five to set his nets.

In the meantime, CJ's shirtsleeves fluttered in the wind like hapless puppets. Jolene squinted out to sea, dropped the wash basket at the foot of the stairs, and climbed back up. The blue white-trimmed clapboard house, set well back from Jeremy Creek, had escaped dozens of storms like this. Ruby would not be the last.

❀

CJ KNEW IT TO be true. He lived for shrimping. And for not much else. He was never so content as when the *Missy Nona* pitched on a rolling sea at sunrise. This morning, ahead of Ruby, shrimpers like CJ were out after brown shrimp in a harvest that had begun in early May, steering clear of the "dead" bottoms. It's common knowledge that shrimp prefer mud to sand.

He'd quit the dock this morning in darkness. But now, short of seven o'clock, the sky had lightened behind the overcast of dawn. Sunrise on a clear day was about the finest part of living, CJ reckoned. On such days, a brilliant orange ball would inch up out of the blackness of the sea, rising into an ever-lightening sky. A metallic dance of light would then reflect on the heaving swells like magic. There was nothing like it.

Beyond the small crew he trawled with, CJ had never been much for company. And they were not with him today. Being alone on the sea, under God's watchful eye, was all CJ could ask for. It pained him to admit it, but he cared more for the herring gulls, the brown pelicans, and the bottle-nosed dolphin that followed in the *Missy Nona*'s wake than he ever had for his late wife and his baby girl. Jolene was a savvy child, he told himself. She didn't need him. Beaus by the dozen trailed after her. Sooner or later, one of them would carry her off.

Deep down, CJ recognized the folly in this. But try as he might, he couldn't change.

Shrimp boats haul their nets within sight of the shoreline, and from a distance, their outriggers resemble a bird's wing or a fish's fin, and a trawler becomes one with the sea. That's just how CJ liked it. Salt water had pooled in his veins from a very early age.

For McClellanville's annual Lowcountry Shrimp Festival, the first Saturday in May, shrimp boats plied the water of Jeremy Creek down to the sea, where churchmen blessed the fleet and petitioned the Lord for a safe and plentiful harvest. At four or five years old, CJ had been decked out in seaman's gear for just such an occasion. And from that day forward, he never again felt steady on his land legs. Shrimping was his life. He would haul back three times a day, at the peak of the season, dumping each catch on the deck. And the crew would separate the shrimp from the bycatch.

But today, alone, CJ had only set a try-net, checked by the half hour to estimate a catch. Today, alone, CJ had other plans. He was headed south, ahead of Ruby, down to Hilton Head or Beaufort—and he wasn't coming back.

🌸

"LORDY, MY GIRL. AIN'T you a sight."

Just short of noon, Mags had pulled Jolene in out of the surge. The winds had intensified, and the girl's hair had been whipped to a stringy tangle, a spit of rain speckling her starched white uniform. The sign over Mags's had begun to bounce and twist from side to side, and the tops of trees up and down the wide street rolled and reeled.

"I reckon we'll shut down early," Mags said mid-afternoon. "An hour or so yet, give or take. Folks'll be hunkerin' down against old Ruby here."

The diner was empty but for Mags, Jolene, and Mags's two cats. The young calico pair, Kahn and Gussie, sat grooming themselves on the café's polished pine countertop, oblivious to the raging storm outside.

The windows had been shuttered. The lights had been dimmed. Regulars had dropped in noon to one, as usual, before the deluge. The room still smelled of freshly brewed coffee and Mags's Monday special—filet of flounder taken from the clear waters of the Southern Outer Banks, battered and fried to a crispy golden brown.

Ruby had let loose. Palmetto heads flailed in ever-widening circles, bending so hard to the west that Jolene thought they would snap. Curtains of rain shifted horizontally across the landscape. As with most things, Mags took Ruby's fury in stride.

"I'm guessin' your daddy's been out on the lines this morning," Mags said. She slipped a checkered apron over netted gray hair and plunked herself on a barstool.

"Yes, ma'am," Jolene answered. She took the seat beside Mags and wrapped her hands around her coffee cup.

"He was off at the crack of dawn," she said. "Like as not, he's tied up wherever the wind blew him in."

Jolene surveyed the empty diner.

"I see you ain't gone whole hog this time around, Mags."

"No—no." Mags waved a stocky hand in the direction of the roadway out front. "I figure old Ruby here's no more'n a pup. They ain't even callin' her a tropical depression no more. I take my measure from Hugo, like always."

Born to McClellanville the same year as CJ, Mags—as Jolene well knew—had her very own Hugo tale.

The village had been ground zero, and the stronger north side of Hugo's eyewall passed directly over the town. With other fleeing townspeople, Mags had taken shelter in the high school cafeteria. Water rose above the tables so quickly that they'd all had to scramble up into the rafters.

Lacking stilts, Mags Diner took on twenty feet of tidal surge after Hugo, leaving the building under eighteen feet of water by morning. They'd boarded up the windows and doors beforehand and removed the outside awnings. But the roof took off early, along with the curlicued *Mags Diner* sign out front and the wooden flower boxes to either side of the main entrance.

When the water receded, the diner's insides were gutted. Half a dozen shrimp boats lay in a heap outside the front door, some of them sheltering copperheads. One live oak, uprooted with a large chunk of the backyard, crushed a neighbor's minivan and took out an electrical transformer that must have exploded like a pipe bomb, had anyone been able to hear.

"Young master Kip pulled in this mornin'," Mags offered with a broad wink. She brushed her cool fingertips across the back of Jolene's hand. "Drove up in that heap of metal he calls a pickup. He says he's off on some inside job up north by Georgetown. Be back this way a-courtin' later on tonight."

Mags sat back with a hearty laugh. "Well—them weren't his exact words, my girl. Ain't likely he'll be back, leastwise not tonight. Not if he's got any brains left in him."

Mags tapped Jolene's arm again.

"I know he's been naggin' on you to slip away with him out west. And you could do worse than to keep company with a journeyman carpenter."

Mags eyed the front door as it rocked and rattled under Ruby's lashing rains. "Keep you from drownin' *here* anyways."

"Ummm." The prospect of a dry life on the road had become ever more appealing to Jolene with each soggy ordeal. "I ain't gonna lie, Mags. It's weighin' heavier on my mind all the time."

"The fact is, your daddy and me, we been friends for as long as the tide's come in." Mags slipped off her stool and retrieved a coffeepot from the far end of the counter.

"Shrimpers got fierce competition these days, don't you know. Foreign imports. Gulf shrimp. Commercial farms. And then them developers been beatin' up and down our shoreline for decades, like a rash of jellyfish. Renovating this. Demolishing that. Tightening up all the dockage. And Lord knows there ain't the shrimp in these waters that there used to be."

Ruby scratched on the roof tiles, rainbands drowning the diner in gusty waves. Magnolia branches cracked like buggy whips against the roofline and windowpanes as Mags topped off their mugs and went back to replace the coffeepot.

"Shrimping's all your daddy knows, my girl," she said, returning to her seat. "He's been in love with the sea, and not much else, for as long as I've known him. A rogue wave, I'd call him. He's worked hard to keep the family above water and hold on to your old place down on Jeremy Creek. Breaks my heart to tell you . . ."

A blinding jolt of lightning cut Mags off, its accompanying barrage of thunder unleashing from the rear of the building. Even Mags jumped.

"Nosy as I am—and the world's my witness—" She hopped off her stool again and made for the back door. "He's had word of foreclosure on the place."

Focused on Ruby's growing violence, Jolene barely heard Mags. An earsplitting explosion rocked the diner, and one more lofty live oak strangled in Spanish moss and wisteria crashed to earth in a heap of brush. The tips of the tree's outer limbs scrapped along the building's eastern wall like gigantic fingernails.

It was time to hunker down like everyone else. And maybe Mags was right. Time to cut bait and run too. A new life in new surroundings was making more sense to Jolene than ever.

❧

THOUGH MAGS HAD SENT them off with a hamper filled with food, north of Shreveport, Kip and Jolene stopped for fried catfish and hush puppies at a tiny shop in Crossroads of Ida. Cornfields, meadowland, and forest lined the roadway, and the skies were clear. Kip was driving, though they'd shared that task since leaving McClellanville three days before, just as the last of Ruby moved inland.

Jolene filled her last Carolina days moving the flotsam and jetsam of her daddy's stilted home into storage in Mags's garage. Once again, the house had risen above the fray. Only Celeste's green laundry basket and a handful of CJ's work shirts had been taken out to sea.

"You call me, my girl, anytime, now, you hear?" Mags made her promise. And from the passenger seat, Jolene had smiled and waved.

CJ had rung up just before they left—dredged in the aftermath of Ruby and conscience. He'd fessed up about the house, about his shrimping woes and Mags's offer to take Jolene in now that they'd lost their home. He said he'd accepted a spot down south in the Beaufort shrimping fleet. He was sorry.

Jolene told him not to fret. She'd meant to leave anyway.

CJ was silent for a moment, and when he spoke again to say goodbye, the relief in his voice was palpable. More power to him, Jolene told herself, staunchly setting her own new course.

Across from her, Kip donned a cap the color of his chestnut ponytail, the visor embroidered with *McClellanville, South Carolina*, in bright red letters.

"Any regrets?" he asked.

"Not a one."

Jolene had known Kip from the day she was born. He'd been with his widowed mother the day Celeste went into labor. CJ was out shrimping. With her two-year-old son, the woman had rushed Celeste to the healthcare center on Tiburn Road, and the families—CJ aside—had been close ever since.

Best of friends start to finish, Jolene thought, smiling into Kip's soft gray eyes. Ever closer to the breathing room of West Texas, to dry roads and a fresh start.

Belle

(A Black Camera Lens Cap)

*From "day's eye," Common Daisy or **Bell**is perennis is the flower of children and innocence, and combines its white ray "petals"—sometimes tipped with red—with yellow disc florets.*

COOPER WAS RIGHT TO use the word "eerie." Suspended in cold gray fog, the Cape held its breath, spooky and silent but for the muted thunder of distant waves.

Two days ago, just before daybreak, Belle had taken the same seven-mile drive from St. John's with her ten-year-old grandson, Cooper. They'd stood mesmerized as the rising sun shouldered itself up from a splendid, primordial sea, saturating the sky with crimson, warm tangerine, and a deep yellow gold. Plumes of spray from humpback, minke, and finback whales had sprouted offshore like tiny fountains, and the frozen sails of June's icebergs drifted silently southward.

Secluded on Newfoundland's Avalon Peninsula, Cape Spear has the distinction of being the most easterly point of land in North America. From the clifftop, Belle had snapped some of her best seascapes, first on the continent to capture the sunrise.

She'd leaned into the rugged morning wind to stay upright, with her arms clamped around Cooper's waist and her tripod and gadget bag slung across her back off the right shoulder. The view was breathtaking.

Atlantic seas roiled against the cliff bottoms. Diving gannets spiraled downward out of azure skies. Belle had been able to see all the way back to Signal Hill, where the entrance to St. John's harbor glowed in anticipation of a new day.

Dusk, she now realized, felt very different. The exhilaration she had experienced with the Cape's blue skies and popping color quickly succumbed to a low-level anxiety that lunged out of the deep-sea mist like a raptor's talons.

Peering through the deepening gloom, Belle shook her head against a creeping apprehension and pulled the tripod from the trunk of her car. "Scout your location," she muttered to herself. "Scout your location."

Her photography instructor in Ottawa liked to emphasize the romance of a fogbound coast. The moodiness and the mystery. But here, alone, Belle felt only a brittle dampness as beady filaments trickled through her short gray hair to dribble down the back of her anorak. She snapped the jacket's hood over her head and hoisted the tripod to her right shoulder. Crossing the parking lot, she continued down the empty boardwalk and started up the long wooden staircase that would bring her to the Cape's two famous lighthouses. Two hundred steps, Cooper had said.

Left and right, the land dissolved into a grayish-white void. Darkened rocks emerged here and there out of the murkiness—most of them bare, others speckled with a thin sporadic layer of moss. Decorated with only the odd fluff of bog laurel or Labrador tea plants, the landscape resembled nothing so much as Arctic tundra. Out of sight, in the clammy dankness, there might be a smattering of black crowberry or blueberry. Even wild rose. But Belle could only guess.

Midway up the staircase, she paused to catch her breath.

And there—just there—drifting in out of the shadows . . . wasn't that a sigh, the barest hint of a muffled sob?

In the next instant, the roar of a breaking wave muted the thought. Belle readjusted her tripod and crept on.

All last evening, Cooper had entertained the family with tall maritime yarns of floundering pirate ships, forgotten cemeteries, murderous wreckers, and the specters of drowned sailors. His favorite tale, which caused Belle to shudder, drew on the burning of the tiny Avalon village of Chance Cove, just south of Cappahayden on the eastern shore.

"Aw, don't worry, Nana. That was way back in the 1880s," Cooper had said. But the tale was too good not to embellish.

"Wreckers probably lured in some ship, dangling lanterns over the cliffs. Everyone on board drowned. And five years later—"

Cooper stretched each syllable to the breaking point. "On the very same night as the old wreck. Bloodcurdling screams. Horrible ghouls."

All the people ran to the beach to see if another ship had run aground and the racket died down, starting up again as everybody left.

"The villagers burnt the whole place to the ground and moved away," Cooper finished, grinning with a deep satisfaction.

"Some pretty gnarly things go on up there at Cape Spear, Nana," he added.

Cooper's eyes narrowed, his voice lowering to a menacing whisper. "Especially after the sun goes down."

"That's enough, Coop! You're spooking your grandma."

Belle's son-in-law, Zane, sprang forward on the sofa to ruffle his son's dirt-blond hair. He turned to Belle with a wink. "By that he just means a handful of juvenile delinquents puffing on joints in one of the old bunkers."

Reeney, Belle's daughter, got up from the couch and headed to the kitchen.

"You'll be fine, Ma," she said, stopping in the doorway. "Just don't wander off the boardwalk. And don't mess about on any of the black rock—that slippery, oily-looking stuff at the water's edge. It's been hit by rogue waves, and it'll be hit again."

Returning from the kitchen, she passed her mother a mug of hot cider. "And don't get too close to the cliff edge. If you stick to the lighthouses, those creepy bunkers, the old ammo batteries—like I said, you'll be fine."

And so she was—at least thus far.

At the top of the stairs now, Belle off-loaded her tripod and splayed out its legs.

Directly ahead of her, obscured by the blanketing mist, rose Newfoundland's oldest surviving lighthouse, a white two-storied wooden structure dating back to 1836.

Belle fitted a wide-angle lens to her camera.

Since her retirement from a prestigious Ottawa accounting firm, Belle had taken up photography, less as an avocation than as a hedge against a widow's loneliness. She'd learned to be patient and observant; to shoot for a changing mood, for the time of day, or for the natural light's intensity, direction, and color. She loved the way she could manipulate storm clouds, shattering waves, or the bare rock and tidal pools of low tide, all into minimalistic arrangements of sand and sea and sky.

A coastline, an oceanfront, a lakeshore.

That was what stirred Belle's soul.

This thick dispiriting fog did not.

She had only come again because Reeney had convinced her that the Cape at dusk would be "more authentic." The brooding atmosphere. The inky water.

But Belle was only cold and wet.

Still, this was her last chance to capture the Cape before heading back to Ottawa in the morning, leaving Reeney, Zane, and Cooper behind in their robin's-egg-blue St. John's cottage.

She snapped a clear filter on her lens. The wild mercurial weather and the shifting winds of the unforgiving Atlantic might put life in some perspective. And besides, Belle wouldn't allow her imagination to get the best of her.

But wait! Wasn't that a shuffle of footsteps? She squinted toward the fogbound lighthouse. Two oblong black windows in the blurred face of the building stared back at her in silence.

Did Cooper really have to bring up the caribou when he was telling his ghost stories? Was it true that the most southerly herd in North America—and perhaps the most menacing—lurked about here on the Avalon?

Belle scolded herself. How likely was it that some clattering beast would come tumbling out of the mist, threading out of the backcountry, to land in her lap?

"Pshaw!" She sighed and bent her head to her work again, affixing the camera to her tripod.

Slow shutter speed.

Wide aperture.

Belle positioned the lighthouse at the top left corner of her shot and let the fog accentuate the structure's lines.

Peering through the viewfinder, Belle gasped. Was her imagination playing tricks on her again?

What was that washed-out filmy figure poised at the rear corner of the building?

She bolted upright and stared at the lighthouse, her breathing now thin, rapid, and shallow. But the shadow, if it had ever really been there, had vanished.

"Balderdash! Get a grip!" Belle said aloud, rather too forcefully for her own jittery nerves. Surely the Cape drew other visitors at dusk. Photographers can't always have a canvas to themselves. And hadn't there been a small silver-blue Volvo abandoned at the opposite end of the parking lot? But still . . .

How many tourists had drowned at the Cape in the last six months? Belle suddenly wanted to ask Reeney. How many old ladies washed out to sea, their camera straps wrapped around their necks?

She fired off a rapid series of shots and detached the camera.

From the rear of the lighthouse, along the cliff's edge, a white picket fence protruded from the mist. Shooting from just past the right crook in the barrier, drawing that fence to the left from the near-center of her shot, Belle just might produce an intriguing, if somewhat spectral, portrait.

Courage renewed and camera in hand, she picked her way along the fence to its far right side. As she leaned a foot or so out over the topmost rail, the lighthouse stood upper left again in her viewfinder.

Directly below, the ground fell away to nothingness. In a gray shroud, beyond the fence, the building wavered in the mist, a convulsion of green-black rock and moss making for a sharp and focused foreground.

That was when she heard it. A rustle. A scraping. A clawing that rushed up out of the mist directly ahead and slid downward again and outward into the awful emptiness.

Startled, Belle's hands flew open, and she watched her camera sail down the cliff face, bouncing from rock to rock, its lens cap flying free.

A heaving recoil raced up out of the shadows, as if the icy Atlantic below had swallowed something far more sinister than Belle's hard-won Canon.

Stumbling from the fence, she swiped her tripod and camera bag from the soggy ground where she'd left them, slung both over her shoulder, and sprinted for the stairway.

Two hundred steps disappeared behind her like water down a drain.

She flung her equipment into the back seat of Zane's old Ford and sped off for St. John's, not slowing until she'd reached Reeney's, where she received a welcome out of all proportion.

❧

"EMERGENCY RESPONDERS ARE at Cape Spear at this hour, following a report of a woman's body in the water. Traffic is blocked at Blackhead Village Road, with no access to the Cape. Officers of the Royal Newfoundland Constabulary have confirmed that there is no sign of foul play, but an investigation is ongoing. Initial reports at the scene point to a suicide."

Verna

(A Jar of Pickled Onions)

In folklore, death follows the picking of the azure Gentian **Verna**—*Gentiana verna—with its slender, bitter-tasting petal tubes. Yet before the introduction of hops, Gentians flavored ales.*

FRANKLY, I WASN'T ALL that surprised when I heard Delaney had gone overboard. They say it was somewhere between Castle Island and Long Wharf, on the *Boston Sea Rover*'s Sunset Harbor Cruise. Verna claims he tripped himself up, and the Boston PD seem to agree. Went over the side slick as a dolphin, pickled onions and all. The deck must have been slippery after an early evening downpour. I'll give her that. Maybe she tried to snag him, and maybe she didn't. Nothing would surprise me there.

Not that I'm a teetotaler or anything, but he was always heavy on the sauce, Delaney. And then Verna, who's been tending bar for years now, whips up a mean Gibson martini. Her signature drink. Delaney's too, I guess. Verna used to tease him about always having a jar of sweet pickled onions on hand, in case of a martini emergency. Back in high school, of course, it was all microbrews and cheap wine.

So you can't necessarily put it all on Verna, like I know some people are doing. Delaney drank himself silly dozens of times. We were just kids then. But once a sot, always a sot, I say.

To tell the truth, Delaney was the best-looking guy around back in the day. Captain of the basketball team, at least for a semester or two, before he got himself expelled. We'd all just started our senior year, him at the hoity-toity Milton Academy, and Verna and I down the road at Milton High. Those MA boys came over our way all the time. On the slum, we used to say.

Delaney wasn't the kind of bloke Verna dated in those days. She hardly dated much at all, and they were leagues apart in so many ways. Everybody knew it. But for some reason, he paid a lot more attention to her than anyone would have thought. I can't quite put a finger on it even now, though I have my suspicions. I don't know if he was playing her back then, or if he was for real. I don't think Verna knows either.

Delaney's family was highborn. The kind of crowd that sails yachts and summers up by Bar Harbor. He was an only child, but as an extended family, they were all fairly well situated—attorneys, doctors, CEOs. Delaney was the black sheep of the lot. Most of the time, he seemed to revel in that. At least he did in high school. And maybe by the time he'd figured out what he really wanted from life, it was too late to climb out of that dark sheepskin and worm his way back into the fold.

In any case, I don't think he was happy about where he ended up. In real estate. Never did reach any celestial heights. I mean, there was no peddling of Boston Celtic mansions or MIT estates. I think of him now as more of a used car salesman, with his slicked-back hair and his too-perfect teeth.

His mother, Prudence, was the catalog trophy wife. We all called her Prude, behind her back, of course. Her life was all hair salons and spas, charity functions and cuticles. I'm not sure she even knew how to boil water. His father, Alistair, the fourth, fifth, sixth—I forget which—was some hotshot corporate attorney.

I saw the inside of their house precisely once. They lived over in Back Bay, in a huge brownstone row house. A three-story affair on Arlington Street close to Park Square. It was a late-summer evening. Cool. Drizzly. I remember that the rosebushes in the piddling front garden had all drooped and faded. Petals all over the place like a wedding gone bad. I thought to myself, *Where the hell's the gardener?* But it ended up Prude did all the gardening herself. Some sort of therapy for her nerves, Verna said. And even then, she hardly got her hands dirty.

Anyway, I don't know anymore why we were even there, beyond meeting up with Delaney. I just remember ringing the front doorbell. A starched Colombian maid, Rosita, opened the door. Verna had told me what little she knew about her on the long, *long* MBTA ride over. Illegal. Humongous family back in Bogotá. Dismal command of the English language. Nice enough, though I don't think she said two words—English or otherwise—while we were there.

There were no crumpets and tea or anything like that, but we were set down in a grand parlor with a huge bay window, looking out on that ramshackle front yard while Prude rustled up Delaney. More dark oil paintings of hoary ancestors hung on the walls than I'd ever seen in one place before. We sat there, poker-straight, on the edge of a brocaded divan. Verna whispered to me a time or two, saying something I never quite made out. Otherwise there was only the dim sense of a clock lopping off the time somewhere in the hinterlands. It felt like with any sudden sound, the facets in the crystal chandelier swaying overhead would fracture.

After what seemed like an hour or more, Sir Alistair—Verna always called him that, though, of course, he was neither knighted nor British—appeared out of nowhere, as stiff on his feet as we were on the couch. To this day I don't recall if he even looked either one of us in the eye. Somehow, I doubt it. He mumbled something about the weather. At least that's how it sounded. And that's how we took it.

"Looks like another bad day," he said . . . and then vanished as creepily as he'd arrived. We talked about it right afterward, Verna and me. We'd both felt Sir Alister's ashy-gray eyes riddling our skulls. I guess in his world, *we* were "another bad day" in the flesh. But we told ourselves he'd really meant the weather. And neither of us ever mentioned it again.

Prude hovered behind him, smiling excessively, until *poof*, she was gone too. So that's the first and the last time I ever saw either of them.

I remember Verna saying there was a messy divorce about ten years ago, with lots of sniping skirmishes over antique Dorasht Persian rugs, two shiny silver Mercedes, and Sir Alistair's bulging stock portfolios. Verna said Prude ended up in some loony bin with a nervous breakdown.

Verna was a whole other kettle of fish. A mousy sort, quiet and unassuming. At least that's how she presented herself to the few friends she had in Milton. She told me once that her grandparents had come from Sicily just after WWII. And she had a sweet-faced little half-sister named Lynette . . . Lindy . . . Leonora. Something along those lines. Verna said she'd woken up from a nightmare in her early teens with Lindy/Lynette's pudgy little hands clamped around her throat. Scared the shit out of her.

Anyway, she had a hard life and a hard family. A whole

different level of pain from Delaney's. She and I were hardly what you would call bosom buddies. She was a bit of a stick-in-the-mud even way back then. And while I wasn't best in show or anything, I did have more on the ball in those days than she did. Her stepfather, Pontus, was some sort of arti-san, a furniture maker. Mostly cabinets, if I remember right. Verna once gave me a letter opener he'd made. A beautiful thing, with a handle of polished oak and maple wedges arranged chevron-like. I still have it.

Pontus had done well in the business, judging from the Milton home they owned down on Eliot Street. As far as I know, they still live there. I stopped by dozens of times over the years, and that house was always neat as a pin, inside and out. The front porch, painted robin's egg blue, was screened with latticework white picket fencing. I always loved the bright salmon-colored azaleas at the top of the rock garden.

Pontus's workshop was in the basement. And whenever I came by, he was usually down there sawing and hammer-ing, hammering and sawing. He'd come up for air a time or two, and then he was all over Verna like a leech, laying into her with what you could only call verbal abuse.

"Washing out in chemistry again this year, eh, Punky?" he'd say with a roll of his inky Italian eyes.

Or, "Apathy never got a single soul anywhere in this life, girl."

Or—and this was his favorite—"Off you go now, Punky. Lindy/Lynette's got a track meet."

Sometimes it was drum-and-bugle-corps practice. Or a ballet recital. Or chess club. Or an ice-fishing contest. Whatever it was, it always trumped Verna.

The girls' mother, Sophia—short, stout, square-faced—was a bit on the naggy side, too, according to Verna. I heard volumes from her myself about the sawdust Pontus dragged up from the cellar on the bottoms of his work boots and deposited all over the maple-wood flooring . . . but never once did I see her badger Pontus about the unfair treatment of his stepdaughter. I always felt a tad sorry for Verna, up against her parents' indifference, living the life of a second-class citizen to the perky and ever-popular Lindy/Lynette.

In the short months before Delaney was expelled, Verna and Delaney became an item. His grades were dismal by then, and hers were no great shakes either. When I look back on it, Delaney's interest in Verna may have only amounted to a *My Fair Lady* thing, given his own more affluent familial circumstances. They wore identical eyeglasses, Verna and Sophia. A pukey tan sprinkled in the corners with flecks of gold. Verna's hair was a deeper charcoal than Sophia's, and she kept her weight down in a way I always envied. Maybe he truly did care about her. Or maybe he just used her to poke a middle finger in Prude and Sir Alistair's collective eye. If Verna had an opinion of her own, she played things pretty close to her chest and never said much about it. But again, I don't think she ever really knew. Maybe Delaney didn't know either.

After graduation, they seemed to fill in parts that were missing in each other. Attention. Appreciation. Acceptance. I still had a sense of them leaning on each other a little too heavily. And in the end, that leaning took on a life of its own. They lost track of who they were separately, as if they'd ever known. I guess they loved each other, at least as much as either of them understood love to be. But they seemed to be floating, treading water. Holding each other's head above water just to keep from drowning.

To be fair, I rarely saw them in those first few years. They had a place down on West Second Street in South Boston. Prude and Sir Alistair never came by even once, so far as I know, though they did—for the sake of appearances,

Verna said—keep them fed and watered, so to speak. Whenever the real estate business went south for Delaney, which was quite often, his parents even paid the rent. From what Verna told me, he never did get the hang of good salesmanship. She took a stab at the nails and hair thing Prude did so well, but it just wasn't her schtick. Instead, she did a lot of light, dead-end store clerking.

Verna said Sophia and Pontus swung by maybe once or twice a year, usually on holidays. Pontus must have gone through some sort of subdued epiphany by then, suddenly more interested in Verna's well-being. He set them up with beautiful cabinets and dressers and bed stands. Probably rejects of one sort or another. But at least he made an effort, which was more than he'd ever done before.

I only ran into Verna and Delaney occasionally in those days, usually at one of the craft beer festivals downtown. They'd invite me to dinner, and, though I hadn't thought of either of them in years, curiosity got the best of me and I'd go.

The last time, just before Halloween, three or four years ago now, I stopped in at about six thirty on a cool, soggy October evening. Verna had arranged a lavish fall display in the flat's spacey "small-town store front" window. She'd tucked crunchy tan corn shucks into each corner, and pushed a bale of hay up against the back wall with a scarecrow on top in coveralls and a straw hat. And then she'd scattered red and yellow maple leaves everywhere. She'd even carved up a set of odd-shaped pumpkins into jack-o'-lanterns, each with a glowing candle inside. I was way more impressed with the window dressing than I was with the lasagna she served for dinner.

When all was said and done, the evening was okay for me, but I detected a widespread nip in the air. Every other line one of them uttered, the other would correct, elaborate on, or contradict, and their efforts to put on a good show started to wear. As the evening crawled to an end, it had turned a lot colder inside than out.

But it was frosty outside too. We all expected snow before I got home, so Verna sent me off with a bulky navy-blue sweater she'd inherited from her mother on her last birthday. I'd get it back to her in a week or two, I promised.

And I did—on a dismal late afternoon in early November.

Verna's Halloween spread still occupied the window space, but the corn stalks and the scarecrow had collapsed into a tangled heap on the floor. Cobwebs quivered in all the corners, and the pumpkins, shriveled like the faces of old men, oozed with fuzzy black mold.

So I wasn't surprised when I learned, just a year or two later, that Verna had reached a limit of sorts with Delaney. She'd pulled herself together and signed up for bartending school. Mixology, she called it. Maybe she'd just had enough of being Delaney's one-time social experiment.

Anyway, when she started slinging whiskey down on Canal Street, I saw her more often. I was working over that way myself by then. She'd had cherubs and rosebuds tattooed up and down her arms, splashed livid lilac highlights in her hair, and had body piercings in places that hurt just to think about. It was like she'd stepped out of herself into something pretty big and shiny.

Regulars dropped in by the dozens, and Verna knew them all by name. Stereotyping, I know, but some confided in her as if she were their best friend or their big sister. She got off on that, I think. Maybe for once in her life, she felt important and useful. Empowered, I guess you'd say.

Actually, that's just about the time she established the stellar reputation I mentioned earlier for her famous Gibson martinis. I'm no aficionado, but Verna's Gibsons are to die for. She varies her vermouth depending on the dryness she's after, and she prefers vodka over gin. James Bond not-withstanding, it's all about the stirring, Verna always says. Carefully and gradually, so as not to over-agitate the ingredients or break up the ice cubes before the concoction is strained into a glass. Garnish with a sweet pearl cocktail onion, pickled with just a hint of turmeric and paprika, and —voila!

Anyway, as it happened, old Delaney's image reflected pretty poorly in Verna's backlit bar mirror by then. He'd grown fat and slippery, she said, perfecting a lazy reliance on his mother's manipulative generosity. No ambition, no initiative. And, all too frequently, no paycheck.

After work, when I'd pop in on Verna's shift, she'd give me the nitty-gritty. More often than not, I'd witness a row myself. They usually started with Delaney's "How's it going, babe?" and deteriorated from there.

From Verna's perspective, things weren't going well at all, at least not so far as she and Delaney were concerned. "Maybe if you'd stop pandering to your mother's every whim, things could be better for us," she'd say.

After she and Alistair divorced, Prude had taken a sudden maternal interest in her only child. After puttering around alone in that rambling Back Bay brownstone for years, barely versed in the changing of a light bulb, she'd been hounding Delaney and Verna to join her in a suite of rooms she'd remodeled on the lower floor. A troll for live-in help, Verna concluded.

"She's just lonely," Delaney would throw back, along with the Gibson martini Verna always handed him as he settled into his barstool.

"Aren't we all," she'd say.

It was always the same argument. "Did you manage that open house down by the waterfront?"

"Bernice covered for me again," Delaney would say, draining his second drink. "I had to hang Mother's new drapes in the dining room."

There was always some new task.

"Took me all afternoon. She wants us over for dinner again Sunday night. I said we'd be there by seven."

"Working," Verna would say. Sometimes even I knew she wasn't.

I didn't see her again for a while, but I knew Verna had been bartending on the *Boston Sea Rover* a little over two months at the time of the accident. Knowing everyone by name down on Canal Street had become tiresome, too set in stone, she told me. She was ready to move on and much preferred the *Sea Rover*'s constant change of faces. I got the feeling she rather hoped Delaney's face would be one of them. She talked about moving to LA or Chicago. But that sounded more like a mantra than anything else.

All too often, Delaney managed the *Sea Rover*'s sunset cruise too. He'd made as much a habit of Verna as he had her martinis.

That night, Verna claims she was up on deck with Delaney at the end of her shift, razzing him as the boat headed back to harbor. Delaney was "in his cups again," as Verna always put it. After two or three woozy lurches her way—waving the nearly empty plastic jar of onions he'd filched from the bar—he threw up over the railing and then slipped right in afterward, like an overfed harbor seal.

"Took the jar of pickled onions right along with him," Verna said.

Talking to the cops was no joke, she'd admitted. But she laughed when she told me.

Glory

(A Nylon Dive Flag)

Morning **Glory**—Ipomoea purpurea—a species of bind-weed, grows in beach sand. Flowers range from delicate pink to vivid lavender.

ADELAIDE SPOKE FIRST.

She said, "Winn, you took me to paradise."

A hiss of embarrassment bounced off the chapel walls and rippled through the room, flicking at the back of my head like one of Winnsome's old scuba fins. In the front pew, Glory's shoulders gave a slight shutter and went limp. The rector had just called for spontaneous testimonials, but Glory could only manage a dismissive heart-heavy wave.

The room coalesced into a deep, collective discomfort. Eyes shifted as if a rattler had been let loose from the vestry. By the grace of God and some fortuitous fore-thought, Glory's wide-brimmed straw hat shadowed her face. She barely moved.

Brave, brave Glory, I thought.

I'm not much of a diver myself, though my husband has chanced a plunge or two in the past. Neither Glory nor I were much for the monthly dive club meetings up there at Adelaide's Eden Café on Barrington. But, unlike Glory, I did wander in a time or two when I'd been down on the water-front. Adelaide, Eden's mid-forties owner, usually buzzed around the room in a short-skirted power suit at least one size too small, her long rust-colored hair free as flames. She radiated a sensuality as juicy and seductive as her neon-red lip gloss, and when the male-dominated dive club was in session, she struck me as honey to a swarm of bees.

Judging from his demeanor, I'd surmised early on that Winn was part of the hive, especially after Glory mentioned the barnacle grip Winn had on having the dive club meetings at Eden's. Glory, as I well knew, suspected this too.

Neptune's Scuba Center—which Winnsome and Glory owned jointly and which Winn managed himself—was up on Quinpool Road on the other side of the Citadel. One of only a handful of such shops in all of Halifax. Why not meet there instead?

I knew just how often Glory had put this to Winn—day after day over the long fifteen years of their marriage and most recently about a half hour before the seizure last Wednesday afternoon that had made Glory his widow. He'd been tinkering with the mantle clock in the upstairs bedroom when Glory heard a clatter and found him collapsed on the bedroom floor.

At fifty-four, Winsome measured a slipshod five foot six, with choppy hair the color of newly dug parsnips. A reedy rail of a man, he bounced when he walked, always sporting cloudy spectacles and a caterpillar moustache.

Do you see a honey man there?

I didn't think so. But my opinion doesn't matter. He must have had a certain something most of us failed to see.

With tearful snuffles and mascara-stained cheeks, Adelaide is still talking, expounding on Winn's "thoughtfulness" and "decency" during their "breathlessly sensual" afternoon romps. A real snake in the grass, if you ask me. A devil in the garden. I try to block the helium squeak of her voice to focus instead on the soppy June day stagnating outside the chapel's east window. After watching another shudder of grief ripple across Glory's back, I file Adelaide under loneliness, under flirtation, under sad-sack morals. Maybe even under addiction.

I trust that Glory has done so too. So far, she's holding her own. But then Luscious steps up. She says, "Winn, baby. I've always loved you."

Behind a wisp of black veil, Glory's eyes must have rolled upward with robust intensity, leaving behind one of her cracker-jack headaches. She reaches up to knead the back of her neck.

Luscious was Winn's first catch. No one, other than their thirty-something-year-old daughter, Breen, expected Luscious to be here. Certainly not Glory.

Luscious had entered the world as Bertie Lucinda. A frisky nickname for a leggy dark-haired beauty, "Luscious" had come into being during Bertie's sorority days at Dartmouth College and stuck. I'd been loosely aware of her semi-obnoxious senior cheerleader presence from my discreet freshman perspective, but I wasn't impressed.

The years since Dartmouth had not been kind to Luscious. She'd bloated up to three or four times the woman she'd once been, her pasty face oily with sweat. Up there at the lectern now, she burbles on about stolen nights of post-divorce bliss, and I cram her likeness into my mind's eye like stuffed sausage. Luscious—a humpback whale of a woman afloat off Peggy's Cove. A finny sucker-faced remora with the visage of Glory's late husband, Winn, pecks here, nibbles there, darting amongst folds of rubbery cetacean splendor. I smile. What else can I do?

The last time I'd seen Luscious, she'd clamped herself down as solid as a church steeple beside the marble font in this very chapel, witness to the christening of Breen's now four-year-old daughter, Elke. Winn and Glory had arrived just as the first driblets of holy water trickled off the squalling babe's head.

At the time, Luscious stood with her back to the congregation. Wearing a silk saffron jumpsuit, she seemed to expand word by word. A shimmering hot-air balloon with legs. Shriveled up beside her, "Papa Winn" had leaned into the carved Purbeck marble basin, the laces of his maroon track shoes undone. He wore a *Truro Bearcats* baseball cap —bill to the back of his head—and a pair of khaki cargo shorts slung so low on his hips I thought they were in danger of forsaking him. Who dresses like that for a baptism?

Are you seeing that honey man yet?

Me neither. But Sedalia did. She speaks next.

"Winn," she blurts out. "You showed me places I'd never seen before."

Five rows ahead of me, Glory's stifled sobs become a tangible vibration against which some of us cough and some of us clear our throats—all of us knowing now that Sedalia means it.

With her younger sister Blue, Sedalia owns the Halifax travel agency Back and Beyond, the very outfit that keeps all of the dive club's foreign outings in working order. Clearly Sedalia had made other, more jaunty arrangements, right alongside the dive site reservations and the wet suit transport.

Sedalia, by the way, isn't a diver. But she prides herself on "specialty tourism" and "soulful experiences." She also travels with her clients, always passing judgment and ruling supreme on accommodations, flight efficiency, and transfer options. All those needling notions the rest of us have so little time for.

I'd have been a dive widow on most of those trips, so

more often than not, I kept to the city, as Glory did. We both lean toward the quick and the painless. I mean, we'd take on short wreck dives at Maugers Beach, for example, on the eastern shore of McNabs Island there in Halifax Harbour. But one sacrificial dawn to dusk penance, and we're back home again.

Now, Sedalia has pulled her long bleached-blond hair into a blue-ribboned ponytail at the base of her neck. Behind her plastic-rimmed glasses, her drizzly green eyes widen and she blinks like an owl. I close up my ears, my eyes, my mind against a litany of "stolen afternoons" I'm convinced Glory has long imagined. Before long, thank God, Sedalia is gone.

At last, I muse, Glory can sit tall. She starts to siphon in a slow and measured breath, and I marvel at how she's kept her composure. But that's just when what remains of her fragile essence collapses with Poppy Jo. "Lolly Pop"—so help me, that's exactly what she says. "Lolly Pop, you were sweeter than sassafras."

Poppy Jo cashiers at Neptune's on Mondays, Wednesdays, and Fridays. Between *college classes*. She must be all of twenty. There's nothing anybody can say to that. I'd called up the shop on my husband's behalf numerous times, frequently getting no response. I'd ask Glory about this at one or another of our quilt club meetings—Neptune's is half hers, after all—and she'd override her skepticism with one of Winn's halting explanations. Loading dock deliveries. Fractious customers. Extended lunch breaks.

I tune Poppy Jo out, but we can all tell that the heat of humiliation has crept up around Glory's eyes and ears. She rocks forward and back with what has to be a venomous, grief-laden distress that punches up and down her spine like a boxer. When she can bear no more, she gathers what little strength she has left and she walks out.

Within a week, one of us will bear witness to Winn's fins, dive flags, and ashes as Glory chucks them off the Macdonald Bridge. And good riddance.

Postscript

Past deadline, but it's in the bag. That's the last good piece of writing I have left in me.

Just last night, a splendid follow-up sprang to mind, and I scratched away far into the night, only to come up with twenty luminous pages that turned to ashes in the light of day.

"You can do this, Erica," Greyson tells me every day.

One of these days, I'm hoping I'll believe again.

FAN GIRLS

A Novella

PART ONE

———

Music gives a soul to the universe, wings to the mind,
flight to the imagination, and life to everything.
—PLATO

THE HOUSE LIGHTS FLARED UP, AND DATHA'S CAPACITY crowd hubbubbed like stunned geese. A sudden snap of light shot out from the row just ahead of me, underscored by a popping sound, and someone screamed. I slumped forward by instinct—we'd all ingested Orlando, the Bataclan Club, Las Vegas, Manchester Arena. My heart pitching into a throat as dry as a mummy's tomb, I locked my eyes on what looked like blood inching across the floor.

But let me back it up.

To bring you up to speed, I have to go back to Datha's last concert here at Chicago's lakeside Midwest Telecom Arena (the MTA)—five months earlier—in late April, when I'd been entertained by the same foursome in that same row.

I don't remember now who came first, though I've a hunch it was Annie Brenner, the weakest link in what I considered some bubble-headed preshow entertainment. A shrug-off to pass the time.

They'd gathered in the row ahead of me, a lob to the left, each unknown to the other so far as I could tell.

Most über fans—myself included—harbor a daydream of some flash or glimmer, tooth or nail, of one band member or another. I'd missed the band's actual sound-check arrival this time around, when, leaning over the lakeside railing, I'd fished out my VIP-package laminate badge from an inside jacket pocket—for perhaps the hundredth time. Somehow it met with the chill of Lake Michigan, lanyard and all, and I had to sprint off to pry another one from the stooge at the VIP desk. No easy task, TBH.

Back in the mingle of zealots at the backstage entrance, I'd heard Annie carp on and on about her ticket, a gift from Raine, Datha's charismatic front man, she claimed. This feather-in-the-cap fired up a klatch of prepubescents who'd lapped it up like hogs at a trough.

To be honest, Annie was credentialed for a legitimate gloat. She'd been chronicled in *Reflections*, a choice Datha bootleg from Chicago, recorded eight years ago at the height of the band's Walls for the Wind Tour. (So twentieth century, I know, but I've burned a DVD myself.) Annie had scored Raine's habitual fan-haul to the stage that evening. This surprised a lot of us. She wasn't exactly hallway queen, if you know what I mean.

The arena doors opened at straight-up seven o'clock, and we were all grateful. April and good weather rarely rhyme in Chicago. I settled in on the pitch, three rows back from center stage. Killer seats, courtesy of Datha.com, the band's official website. For presale to the online fan club, they routinely block the first three rows of each and every venue they play. Front, sides, and back, if necessary.

A black-clad road crew swarmed over the stage and back around the soundboards like termites, and a slew of sparkies tinkered with electrical cables, slapped patching lights on dimmers, and rewired fixtures. Rigging lights flashed with the rhythm of spastic fireflies, and black wires snaked across the floor to titanic-sized thuds that reverberated through the buzz of expectation like jet aircraft breaking the sound barrier. Riggers scrambled up ladders, hauled ropes, maneuvered booms and lifts and hoists. Water bottles sprang up here, a stack of white towels there. Lights and amps and smoke pots. Graeme's guitars were strummed, Dirk's drums manhandled, and someone tweaked all the floor speakers and microphones. "One-two, one-two. Testing . . . testing."

When I stood up to absorb the crowd, a sea of faces stretched up to the rafters, their eyes glinting like bush babies.

In some sense, the four women in front of me mirrored any other hard-core Datha fan at the center that night. Annie may have come first, but Emily Richards sparked my initial interest. She'd swept her short, choppy, nut-brown hair over a wicked bluish-black bruise on the left side of her porcelain face. A fragile countrified earth mother in her late twenties, Emily emanated a disconnect, as though she'd never before encountered such sights and sounds, the crowd and the clamor. She smiled a lot, sweet and breathy, her pale lips curled up like a small-town Mona Lisa. She soaked up the chaos with a down-on-the-farm innocence, which, as it turned out, came from rural Ohio.

Beside Emily sat Dana Morrison—short, tough, foul-mouthed, in black tights, a black leather skirt, and a blue denim jacket embroidered on the back with DATHA, the band's rose-red logo. Her thick-lashed blue-gray eyes had a crystalline quality that I liked, and her short sugar-blond hair, peppered with gray, framed a flawless heart-shaped face a tad on the icy side.

Everyone within earshot and beyond—including the band—knew Dana, the editor of Datha's longest-lived fanzine, *Conversations*, out of San Diego, now in its tenth year online. Dana could boast a factual friendship with Raine, and perhaps because of this we'd all heard a raft of innuendo about her, most of it prickly and much of it cruel. She was "huffy," "overbearing," "pushy." Fans bitched about her swagger, about her puffed-up barbed-wire personality. "Wears life like a pair of itchy jockey shorts," a mutual acquaintance once said. I'd reached out to Dana on occasion in connection with the fanzine—text messages, e-mail, Facebook, Instagram, Snapchat—but we'd never met in real time, and I found her articulate, practical, and self-assured.

Beyond a minor right-leg limp and a habit of crimping tufts of her lackluster brown hair between her forefinger and thumb, nothing much standoutish attached itself to Annie beyond an enormous multicolored woolen poncho she whipped off as she sat down. Thirtyish and mousy, Annie gushed a lot, in awkward limpid spurts. Not over Datha's good looks or music. Not even over her sensational—and highly suspect—snatch of that concert ticket. Rather over some ultra-heavy personal "thing" she had with Raine. "Special" was a word she used to excess, as in "What we have together is *very special*." I remember I rolled my eyes a lot.

Chelsea Davis, the last of the pack, soaked up Annie's rhapsodies with the abandonment of a lost puppy. Her wide blue eyes reflected all the innocence and awe of a child hearing fantastic bedtime stories. Chelsea belonged to a pool of fan-club devotees from Toronto's college-based Gold Rush who'd banded together for the drive over.

Chelsea was retro-hippy. All the right eco-thoughts, green energy to renewable this and that. All the right social mores—refugees to gay rights. An art major, I guessed. Pegged the sort right out of the gate—the ash-blond, poker-straight hair, the wire-rimmed glasses, the tattooed peace symbol on the baby-pink inside flesh of her left wrist. My mind zeroed in on her sailing westward in a flowered VW minibus. I just knew she was a vegetarian.

I can rattle all of this off to you now because I eavesdrop. A lifelong habit, for good or bad, and I'd sensed a story brewing even then.

ii

"TOTALLY CHILL!" CHELSEA PUNCHED BACK HER GLASSES and thwacked Annie's shoulder with the heel of her hand. "What was it like—being pulled up onstage like that?" She unleashed a guttural sound I could barely pick up. Something between a wheeze and a gasp.

"Well, yeah." Annie's eyes, dark and unsettled as windblown sand, shifted, and she curled a swatch of hair middle to forefinger. "Me and Raine go back a long way. My dad's in the Air Force, and he was stationed in England years ago. So I practically grew up there. I spent the summers in Edinburgh with my mom. That's where we really got to know each other."

Chelsea beamed and behind Annie's back, I smirked.

"I don't tell many people," Annie went on, with a "beat-that" snicker that said otherwise. "It's such a personal thing, and it's not so easy for us to be together anymore. But that Walls concert fell on my birthday, and he'd promised me a dance."

On the far side of Annie, Dana winced, propped a black-booted foot on the back of the empty seat in front of her, and fired up a cigarette. My own eyes rolled up into the rafters.

"We must play that video five or six times a year," Chelsea said. "It's so inspiring. Did you see Raine throw Dana a kiss when they went in to sound check?" she asked Annie. Another reluctant smile played over Dana's lips before she hopped over the back of her seat—narrowly missing my own booted foot—and disappeared.

"Emily saw him, didn't you, Em?" Chelsea said. "Em's from Apple Creek, just this side of Akron. This is her *very first Datha concert*. All of this"—she flounced a hand at the seething crowd—"this is just for starters, Em. You must get backstage all the time," Chelsea gushed, swiveling back to Annie. "And over to their hotel? We were there till three o'clock last night. The Park Hyatt on Michigan. Graeme finally came out and signed my *Drift* album. I've got three of him now."

As Dana slipped back into place, Chelsea tweaked her

sleeve. "This is Emily Richards, Dana. This is her *very first Datha* concert. A killer vibe for the 'zine, eh?"

"Hey." Dana dipped her head Emily's way and tapped out another cigarette from a packet she'd pulled up from the breast pocket of her jacket. "I don't mean to be rude, but I lived with a bastard who did that to me once—just once." She slipped the smoke between her lips and lit up.

Emily fingered the welt on her face. "Oh, this." She laughed. "My boy Callum plays baseball. We were just messing around, you know, and I was standing too close to the mound. Got the bat tip square in the face. What a klutz. Shane's always telling me."

"Yeah—right." Dana tossed off her spent match with a flick of her wrist and clamped her foot back on the forward seat.

"There are songs on this last album that I just can't get enough of." Emily grazed a slim hand across her lap. "'Saying Two Things at Once.' Don't we all." She raised an eyebrow. "And 'Full Moon on a Dark Night'? All about hope?" Even I heard the catch in Emily's throat. "There always has to be hope, don't you think?"

"'*Three Candles*' is totally dope," Chelsea tossed in. "'Small Change' is *my* fav. Little things really do add up, don't they? We're gonna go busking for Toronto's Literacy Advocates. Gold Rush, I mean. For small change, eh?" She let out a short staccato yelp like a wounded puppy. "There's this new guy in the group—Nicki. Trustifarian, big-time. Plays harmonica. We'll go over to the Eaton Centre or maybe down on Yonge Street. We're still working out the kinks. I play guitar, and the twins, Stephi and Sam"—she flung a hand in the direction of a gregarious duo two rows up—"they have singing voices to die for. They're my best friends," Chelsea went on. "Well . . . roommates really. We'd do some Datha, too, of course."

"Gold Rush's activism does put a classy spin on the band," Dana said, and catching security, she crushed her cigarette underfoot. "You've avoided the glitz and pretense that comes with so many fan groups. Datha doesn't need any more holy orders or wayside shrines."

"Gee, thanks." Chelsea's eyes widened out of all proportion, and her baby face glowed. "Oh, I brought that poem I wrote about in my last e-mail." She wrestled a crumpled envelope from a hip pocket of her blue jeans, her eyes flitting from face to face. "I call it 'Let it Raine.'"

Emily half smiled. Annie scowled, and Dana's face remained expressionless. I myself choked on my lemonade.

In the next instant, Annie had pulled herself surprisingly tall in her seat and leaned forward. "Raine would love it," she announced. "He's really into poetry. I just gave him a book he asked me to look up for him when I was backstage in St. Louis last week. He's making arrangements for me to stay in Scotland until they're back in the States come September."

"He's what?" Dana and I lurched forward in unison.

But it was too late. The lights dropped. The stage darkened. And the opening chords of "Speaking Eyes" slid over a tumultuous roar.

iii

NO ONE OPENED FOR DATHA. EVER. A PINS-AND-NEEDLES shimmer of midnight blue washed over the stage as the band members slipped into place one by one—Graeme, Dirk, and Colin (Datha's bassist)—each a flat, black shadow in a snow globe of dancing light. Everyone tracked Raine's silent stride to center stage, where a single misted spotlight snatched him up, and when the shrieks and shouts, the hoots and cheers reached hysterical proportions, he waved once, detached a microphone from its stand, and launched into "Speaking Eyes."

iv
—

OF COURSE, IT WAS ALL OVER MUCH TOO SOON. THE celebration. The power. The passion. Datha's final number, at the end of their second encore—"Full Moon on a Dark Night"—expanded into an electrified darkness punctuated by the thousand pinpricks of upraised smartphones. The afterglow lingered long after the band left the stage and the house lights came up. From a bank of speakers to either end of the stage, recorded uilleann pipes dropped down on the buzz and glare of the spent crowd.

We pledged to meet again, right here at the MTA, on the fall leg of Datha's US tour. Dana would see to tickets.

Well, actually, *we* didn't pledge. *They* did. Chelsea, Dana, Annie, and Emily. But I didn't think they'd mind if I came along.

PART TWO

———

Each player must accept the cards life deals . . . he or she
alone must decide how to play.
—VOLTAIRE

Emily's Story

(In Her Own Words)

i

IN THE GRAY DAWN OF EARLY JUNE, I LAY AWAKE, MY eyes closed, my body tensed. I regulated my breath like a string of sighs, mimicking the relaxed, impassive rhythms of deep sleep. Shane was awake too. I could feel his thick, overheated body rolling against my back.

We'd had sex close to three a.m.—a dry, distasteful assault that bore only the faintest resemblance to lovemaking. The shift and weight of him on my chest, my abdomen, my thighs, had been insufferable, and his breath reeked of alcohol. His hands, grainy as sandpaper, ground across my breasts, down along my hips, and between my legs, and when he entered me, his body arched with a string of hammered thrusts, the upshot of which was so unproductive that he'd slapped me across the face, heaving up a slur of words, "frigid bitch" among them.

At first only the sound stunned me—a bristle of static in my left ear and a sharp crack almost like gunfire. My chin jerked over my right shoulder as Shane's whiskied breath bore down on me. I detached from the white heat that now stung my left cheek and crept a hand up to shield my face, knowing that the imprint of Shane's hand now stenciled my skin. Tears climbed into my eyes, and when I swallowed, squiggles of pain pulsed through my blurred vision.

Shortly after that, Shane's face softened above me, and he squinted as if seeing me for the first time. I watched the play of his lips as he begged forgiveness—which I always gave, out of cowardice and habit. And then he fell asleep again.

In the black hole of such nights, withered and broken, my mind grasped at what I called prayer, though I suppose it was actually hope. There always had to be hope. *A Full Moon on a Dark Night.*

Shane left me alone, though I still couldn't sleep, and at close to five a.m. three roosters in the Baxter farmyard next door crowed through the flush of dawn—three times apiece, and then once in unison. By half-five, a gentle cooing and a flurry of wings under the eaves told me that the mourning doves were awake. A bluster of crows swept across the neighboring cornfields, and moments later, despite my exhaustion and despair, I warmed to a new day, got up and set the alarm for seven thirty, lest Shane oversleep, an infraction for which I knew I would dearly pay.

A scalding shower purged my body of his very existence. A scrub, a scour, and he slipped down the drain of matrimonial blunder like mildew. The fresh scent of new beginnings left me unblemished and whole, at least until I stepped out of the tub and met with the wispy image in the bathroom mirror—the anemic eyes, timid as a dormouse's, flat as pools of rain water; the stringy arms; the thin legs. A battered body too slight, too puny, too tired. Shane was too big. I was too small. Some nights there was no moon at all.

Shane lay hunkered under the covers as I dressed. I passed him in silence and went down to the kitchen to start his breakfast. At five minutes to eight, just as I came in from fetching the morning newspaper from the street end of the driveway, he lumbered into the room without a word and slumped down at the kitchen table in the high-backed chair nearest the back door. When I topped off his coffee mug and went back to the stove, homey breakfast smells began to waft through the room.

"Don't keep them damn kids in bed past nine again, Em." Shane shook out the paper without looking up. "I don't give a hoot in hell what kind of excuses they come up with —Saturday . . . school's out. That yard's gotta get cut. And all that shit out there by the garden, that's gotta get cleaned up." He snapped the newspaper back on itself and hunched over the table. "Place looks like a goddamn dump. That trash better be gone when I get home tomorrow night," he said, slurping his coffee and holding up his cup for more. "You're too soft on 'em, Em."

"Hmmm . . ." I nodded and refilled the cup, glancing at Shane's broad face.

He was a big man, heavyset, especially across the shoulders, still handsome in a bleary, shadowy sort of way. His dark hair, slicked into a high '50s shine, had a touch of gray at the temples, but his chestnut eyes had hardened years ago, as if a light had gone out in them.

A lifetime ago, when he was a high school football hero, all sparkling eyes and bronzed skin, and I was a freshman, gangly as ragweed and just as useful, his swaggering self-confidence had fascinated me.

Not once had we spent any time together in those days. He dated prom queens, cheerleaders, and the like. But all through the summer, ninth grade to twelfth, I'd peddled quart baskets of raspberries around the neighborhood. This had thrown me up on the Richards' front porch time and time again. Mrs. Richards and I took to baking rhubarb-raspberry tarts in her kitchen. She liked me. I know she did. She'd pull me out like a paper doll and set me up on some pedestal for Shane and his older brother, Liam, to contemplate. Called me "princess." What a fine farmer's wife I'd make, she'd say. What a fine cook. What a fine seamstress.

When what she was really after was grandbabies from the farmer's daughter she'd never have. For some reason she didn't see them with a pom-pom queen. They barely noticed me, Liam and Shane. And yet sometimes I could hardly see Shane for the glow in my own eyes. He was a phantom, a star in some distant galaxy.

All of that changed when Shane's family died, Liam in a threshing mishap on his twenty-first birthday, both parents sixteen months later, mid-December, when Shane overslept and Lucinda and Devon were forced to take themselves off in an ice storm to a Sunday service from which they never returned.

In a moment of weakness, Shane allowed me to step in and fill the void. I was seventeen, his lost mother's princess. Three months later, two months pregnant, we were married. How could I, so very young, and so very naive, even begin to comprehend the depth of Shane's guilt and shame, the faults and failings that now smothered his heart?

"Them damn Foresters out of Lima," Shane was saying. "They got another claim in for that goddamn tractor of theirs." He shook out the paper as if ringing a chicken's neck, and I slid a plate of food in front of him. Five strips of bacon, crisp but not black, three eggs, over easy with the yolks soft but not runny, two scoops of cottage fries the color of watered whiskey, and a stack of lightly buttered white toast.

"Flood damage," he said. "Can you believe it? Damn piece of shit's so rusted you could use it for a sieve. Flood damage, my ass." He began to eat, drained his coffee mug and held it up for more, and I fetched a freshly brewed pot from the counter.

I've never yet forgotten when the man I thought I loved had disappeared—a scant twenty-four hours after we'd exchanged vows. We were living on Dunstone then, the family farm Shane had inherited.

"Maybe you're just not the farming type," I'd suggested. Out on the tractor most of the morning, he'd come in from the fields for lunch. The scrunch of his face and the whiskey on his breath told me things had not gone well. "I mean some people just don't take to the land like others."

"Like Liam? Like my old man? Like your brothers?" He'd hurled his coffee mug across the room then, leaving a clump of ceramic shards in a puddle at the base of the fridge. Until that moment, I'd only witnessed his temper in words. With the shattering of that glass, all the windows and doors of my life slammed shut tight as a coffin, and the first flickers of fear curled up at the base of my throat. When I reached to brush his cheek, he'd snapped up my wrist, twisting my arm until tears gushed into my eyes. "What would you know about it anyway?"

I'd swallowed hard and backed away, kneading my bruised arm. "I know how hard farm work can be," I said. "I grew up on a farm, too, remember?"

"You think I'm stupid? You think I don't know what people say?"

"People don't say anything."

"What do you tell your brothers anyway?"

"I don't tell them anything."

"What the hell have you told those fucking bastards anyway?" When I couldn't answer, he'd hit me—a searing blow across the right cheek. The memory still makes me queasy.

"Damn Ford's on the fritz again," Shane was saying, more to himself than to me. "Things keep going like this, and those kids'll be out on their butts right out of high school if I have anything to say about it." And Shane always did.

I went back to the stove to whip up a single scrambled egg for myself.

I'd be thirty-two in early September. Shane had turned thirty-five last January. Yet his brutality could still warp me into a dull and inconsequential child. I knew nothing about adjusting insurance claims—Dunstone had gone to back taxes ages ago—and I couldn't have mended his sick old Ford to save my life. My house just never quite blossomed the way Shane's mother's had.

I settled on the lip of the kitchen chair opposite Shane. Chewing on my lower lip, I arranged the sugar bowl, the salt and pepper shakers, the butter dish, my own coffee mug, each of them by turn on the checkered tablecloth. Edges touching a white square. Edges touching a red. Sweat prickled my palms, and I scrubbed them together over the steam from my cup.

From "Speaking Eyes" on, Datha's Chicago April concert had reawakened lost dreams. (I'd raised the possibility of a solo visit to my sister Jessie and her husband in Cincinnati as my cover. In an unguarded moment, Shane had agreed.) Datha's words and the power of their music had ignited a glimmer of my own potential. Isolation melted away with an intensity so intoxicating I could still ball it up in my fist like lightning. I'd stretched my soul out into the glittering darkness, released from expectation, from dependence and fear, determined that whatever threads still held together the thin fabric of my existence, being beaten could not possibly be one of them.

"There's a job opening over there at The Green Leaf, Caitlin says. You know, Ira Grimsby's nursery in Wooster?"

Shane's eyes narrowed.

"I'm good at growing things, Shane. I could work there, just a little while. You know. Save something up for the kids." My scalp tingled, and blood swooshed in my ears like a giant bellows.

When Shane's fist slammed the tabletop, coffee sloshed over the rim of my cup, scalding my hand. "The hell you will," he said. "It'll be a cold day in hell when Shane

Richards can't look after his own damn family. What do you know about that kind of shit anyway?"

My stomach lurched.

"All you do is put up a goddamn hoard of half-rotted apples every fall. And slave over them fucking elderberry bushes out back like maybe they was worth the mess you make of the place."

"I only thought . . ."

"You didn't think, Em."

I tried to stand, but my legs buckled.

"That's always been your problem, Em. You don't think. Never have. Never will."

I held my breath and stared hard at the tabletop.

"Never thought about how things looked last week when you had that Reynolds kid in to do the floors. Half your age, Goddamn it. Half your age. Where do you get these goddamn schemes anyway? My old man had to put up with the same shit." He sprang to his feet, toppling his chair behind him. "Women," he hissed. "Where the hell are them goddamn kids anyway?" He ripped a gray twill suit jacket from the back of the adjacent chair and flung it over his shoulder. "Caitlin this. Caitlin that. You can tell that nosy bitch she can go to hell. If she'd been half the woman she should have been, she'd still be making a decent home for Ted and the kids instead of off there in Wooster, working at the bank."

He was at the back door now. I followed, still shaking, and handed him his briefcase.

"I'll call if I get a chance."

I knew he never would.

ii
—

THE NEXT WEEKEND, AS THE OLD FORD DWINDLED DOWN the road, I rinsed Shane's breakfast dishes and arranged them by size in the dishwasher. I'd not yet gathered the courage for round two, but at least the seed of The Green Leaf had been planted. That the job remained open at all— for over a month now—surprised me, and I took this as a hopeful sign. I collected the three hard plastic scissor-cut shards of Datha's *Three Candles* CD from the living room floor, laid them on the kitchen counter, and had just snapped open a fresh plastic bag for the garbage bin when Callum slouched into the room just short of nine o'clock.

"So the bastard's gone?" He met my gaze with a blend of disgust and defiance. I set a cereal bowl and a box of Cheerios on the tabletop and went back to the sink.

At fifteen, Callum's reedy body mirrored my own, but for his height, which was more than Shane's six feet. He lounged in the doorway now, tossing a baseball overhead, catching it behind his back with a gloved hand.

I slipped the remains of Datha into the trash can.

"Let me guess," Callum said, slumping down at the table, his jean-clad legs stretched out left and right. "That Datha CD you just bought, right?" He grimaced. "Ha! The old fart's tone-deaf too. Can't stomach the sound of any decent music. That country shit of his sucks swamp water."

I laughed, a spunky sound that startled even myself.

Callum's dark eyes widened.

"Your father wants the lawn done," I said.

"I just mowed it last week. What's he want, a fifties buzz on the place?" Hunched over the table, he dumped cereal into the bowl, leaned back in his chair, and threw up his arms. "So where's the milk here, Ma? I gotta eat this stuff raw?"

I nudged a jug of milk from the fridge Callum's way. "You know how he'll be if he gets home and it's not done."

"He's gonna be like that anyway, so what's the big hairy deal. I got baseball practice. Let shrimp do it."

As if on cue, Kit skulked into the room with a dyspeptic "not me." A sequined jumpsuit trailed behind her, pant cuffs dusting the floor.

At twelve, Kit, petite and fragile, shared her brother's wiry frame, my own dust-blue eyes, and Shane's auburn hair.

"I'm not doing it, you pervert," Kit said. I took the ice-skating outfit she held out to me. "And I always have to change the cat box. Let's see you do that for once, toad-breath. It's ripped on the shoulder," she told me.

"Well, fix it," I said.

"What?' Kit pursed her baby-fine lips, and Callum's spoon froze midair. They eyed me as though someone marginally unpleasant had just entered the room. But the moment passed.

Kit sat down opposite her brother and kicked her slippers off so that one of them slapped against Callum's shin.

"Cut it out, Kit," Callum barked.

"Okay, that's it. Both of you. I don't care who does what, and I don't care when, so long as it's all done before your father gets in. Sort it out, the two of you. *I* want this done. And *I* want it done *now*."

By the sudden silence, I'd shocked them. I smiled, relishing how fierce this made me feel.

"That garden stuff was Dad's idea," Kit ventured. "He started it."

"Well, you finish it."

I knew, even before I left the room, that without my asking, Callum would pop his bowl in the dishwasher, and Kit would wipe down the table.

iii

LATE JULY, AND SHANE WAS ON THE ROAD AGAIN. HE'D LEFT his usual weekend orders, and early Saturday afternoon, Callum cut the grass. Kit weeded, pruned, and watered for nearly two hours, and now garden trimmings sprouted from three oversized trash bins in the alley behind the garage. Rakes, spades, and clippers had been returned to the garden shed.

I was glad of it. Summer rains always bring a glut of greenery to Ohio, and any looming yard work undone would only mar the sole slice of serenity I could count on.

Sunlight splashed off the kitchen table's red-and-white checkered tablecloth and fired up the buckled linoleum floor, leaving my spirits elated. With Callum off to baseball practice on the Baxter farm, and Kit ice-skating at Parker's—the combination ice rink and hardware store west of the old mill—I'd rummaged out Datha's most recent CD, *Drift*, from a bedroom dresser drawer where I'd managed to keep it hidden from Shane. The band's exuberant sound showered the room with hopeful possibility.

Were you there when I wanted to fly? Were you the light when I touched the sky? Speaking eyes.

I'd already washed and sorted three quarts of Bing cherries for the freezer. I'd peeled and chopped several dozen rhubarb stalks rescued from a handful of patchy plants inside the backyard gate. Each summer, Shane threatened them with extinction. Remarkably, they'd survived yet another year.

As I worked, long even rows of summer corn outside the window in the Baxter's south-side field rolled like water on a distant sea, and bulky cylinders of freshly mown hay studded adjacent fields. My window boxes mushroomed with coleus, violets, and begonias.

How I treasured the velvet dampness of black loam

crumbling in my hands. Spring earth sliced with fresh shoots as snappy as wintergreen, autumn's crunch and rustle, the chilled sea greens of deep summer—those long sunlit afternoons when sweet peas popped like limey jewels into colanders and new potatoes cracked the earth like nuggets of gold. However small the plot, I always had the land, rich earth to handle and hold, as reliable as the steel-blue hyacinths that bloomed on my bedroom windowsill each year, even as frost still etched the glass.

From childhood, the land had cradled my aspirations. Time had blunted the darker edges of memory. My mother's passivity and disapproval, for example. I don't ever recall her addressing me by name. It was never "Emily" or even "Em." Always "Mouse," or more often, "Skinny Minnie." The only advice she'd ever shared with me was this: "The man is the head of the woman, as Christ is the head of the Church."

Neither of us had had much luck with that. To this day, my mother lives her life as subservient to *my* father as she had been to her own. With all my heart, I'm convinced she was glad when I finally left home. I reminded her too much of herself.

Each of my older brothers, with three flaxen-haired children apiece, worked their hundred-acre farms, one to either side of the Winesburg bypass south of town. Frank's matronly Jeanine and Aaron's bubbly Kate had slipped into place like ducks in a pond.

But me . . . I'd lost everything.

At the age of thirty-seven she knew she'd never drive through Paris with the wind in her hair, a song from my distant past once told me. All my life I'd lived variations on that theme, and I knew better than anyone that I'd never walk the streets of Paris. Nor did I really want to.

But maybe—just maybe—there was still time for wind in my hair.

Into the midst of this reverie, Caitlin Covington cracked open the back deck's screen door and poked her head inside just as I flipped down the oven door and a fruited sweetness drenched the room.

"Coast clear?" Caitlin grinned. "Mmmm. That's just about the finest rhubarb pie on God's green earth, Em. Let's eat the lot of it. Right here. Right now."

In the string of ranch-style houses that reached out into the countryside east of town, ours was the last before the Baxter farm. Barkley Brothers Auto Repair Shop and Pool Hall, a piece of small-town Norman Rockwell, stood directly across the street. Four doors down from there, a trim residential complex housed Cait's tiny townhome. She'd off-loaded an abusive used car salesman three years ago and now worked as a bank teller in Wooster, just to the northwest. Cait's Erin and Seth were schoolmates to Callum and Kit.

A willowy woman of Georgian/Irish descent two years my senior, Cait came with a glut of rust-red hair, emerald eyes, and—on weekends—a pair of snug-fitting blue denim jeans. Her resilience and pizzazz underscored my own timidity, and yet she inspired me with her optimism and self-confidence. We'd met at a Little League game, in the midst of her recent divorce, when she'd challenged as "appallingly inappropriate" the public lambasting of a ten-year-old outfielder.

To Shane, of course, Cait was an affront to right living. "Loose," "mouthy," and "ill-mannered" were the less florid epithets he'd hurled her way over the years.

Cait leaned against the fridge, her feet crossed at the ankles, her ears tuned to the sound of Datha filtering in from the other room. "Oh, that's fine," she said, and stepped over to fill the teakettle at the sink. "How in God's name did you keep *that* out of Shane's hands?" She plugged the kettle in a counter outlet and picked up *Drift*'s jewel box from the tabletop. "*Are yours the hands that laid my fear?*" she read aloud. "Hmmm."

I laughed and placed one strawberry-rhubarb pie on the cooling rack.

"Oh, don't tell me you haven't had any saucy thoughts yourself, what with Attila the Hun after you day and night."

I shook the excess water from the last of the rhubarb stalks and dumped them on the drainboard. "It's the words, Cait," I said. "It's the words . . . and the power in the music. They help me stay hopeful and strong." I dropped two hefty peppermint tea bags in a Brown Betty teapot and sat down.

"Well, now, let me tempt you just one more time with another itty-bitty advert for that job opening at The Green Leaf." Cait pulled out the chair opposite mine. "Starts in the fall, remember? Someone who knows a lot about plants. A 'youngish woman.' God's truth, that's exactly what old Ira said, though it *is* mostly women who go in there," Cait added, by way of explanation, and sat down. "So . . . nine to three. No weekends. Kids in school. What's not to like? It's got your name stamped all over it, Em."

I got up and poured the kettle's contents into the teapot. Taking my seat again, I positioned the teapot, the sugar bowl, the creamer, all of them in a straight line across the tabletop. My insides churned like a sea squall, and a rush of nerves tightened my chest. "How would I get there?" I said.

"I can read you like the Sunday paper, Em. You're angling for any excuse now. You'd drive over with me, of course. We're not talking Gotham City here. I could spit at you from the bank. Not that I ever would." Cait's eyes widened. She got up, skimmed a finger in the cooling pie, and licked it clean. "Like I said, you'd take care of all the stock. You know, keep everybody fed and watered. Pay's good too. Fifteen dollars an hour for starters." She tapped my arm as she sat down again. "You're the right person, Em. You know you are."

"What'll Shane say?" I mumbled, raising an eyebrow. "Never mind. I know exactly what he'll say." I fetched two matching flowered mugs from the cupboard, sliding one Cait's way. Rising steam tinged the air with minty freshness when Cait poured. "He gave me his answer again this morning. Same as April's, only darker."

"You've *got* to get *out* from *under* that man," Cait intoned. "And I mean that literally. You *can* make it on your own. I don't care what kind of grief he gives you, or how hard he works to make you feel small or stupid or worthless. You have to dream, Em. Isn't that what the song says?" Cait motioned toward the music still floating in from the other room. "Think of it. Maybe even your own shop someday. But you have to be alive to do it."

My eyes drifted off over the Baxter cornfields as Datha launched into the positivity of "All That Is"—*From the final flash of day, you stood silver in the wind, like blown glass.* My back garden stretched out its open arms to me—honest, direct, uncomplicated. All my hopes and dreams in long lines of rich black soil.

"I'll do it, Cait," I said, my heart hammering. My fingers grazed the stippled bruise on my cheek. "I'm dying here. I can see that now. I'll tell him when he gets in from work tomorrow night. Before I lose my nerve."

"And think of the kids."

"Shane would never hurt Kit or Callum."

"Oh, well, that's alright then." Cait threw up her hands. "Let him beat the hell out of their mom. It's not right for anyone to carry on the way Shane does. You'd think you had every one of them Datha boys locked up in the basement." She laughed, a soft sultry sound that made me smile. "And look how Callum and Kit treat you. Shane's shown them exactly where you stand. They pick up on that like fleas to a dog. You've got to get out, Em, before it's too late."

"How do I start, Cait? I just can't leave one black hole for another."

"Well, first off, you've got your parents," Cait said, topping off our teacups. "Sorry." She raised a hand. "I take that back. Any man who *makes* his wife color her hair is not a good fit for the twentieth century, much less for this one. You'll stay at my place, of course. Long as you want. Long as you need to. Plenty of room."

"I should talk to him one more time," I said. "He'll go crazy if he comes home and we're all just gone."

"That's what Ted's old Colt 45 in the closet is for."

"I just think I have to try to reason with him one more time. Convince *myself*, I guess, that this is the right thing to do. Besides, I don't have the job yet."

"No, but you will." Cait's certainty buoyed my spirits. "Besides, the job's not the thing anymore," she said. "It's your life. And the lives of your children. In fact"—she sprang to her feet—"let's go on over to Wooster this very minute. See what old Ira's got to say. We'll be back long before any of the kids get in."

iv

THE GREEN LEAF, A LUSH ACCUMULATION OF EVERYTHING I loved most in life—beyond my children—spread out on the outskirts of Wooster like a small-town Garden of Eden. Row on row of shade trees and fruit trees—Ohio buckeye and black tupelo, alder, ash, and pawpaw; Suncrisp and Goldrush apple trees, Potomac plum and black cherry; greenhouses brimming with herbs from anise and basil to tarragon, oregano, and thyme; and garden plants from alyssum to zinnias.

For years, I'd stopped by The Green Leaf on a somewhat regular basis—spring and summer, in search of seed packets and bedding plants, fertilizers and garden tools. Even autumn and winter weekends, when Shane was on the road and the nursery was sometimes technically closed, Ira and I would sip hot chocolate and shop-talk around his pot-bellied stove, comparing border plants and windbreaks.

No doubt he considered me a pleasant enough woman a year or two younger than his eldest daughter, Lydia. And in a neighborly way—in terms of the weather, the county school board, or that business of the footbridge over Schneider Creek—we knew each other fairly well. His grandson Paul played on the same Little League team as Callum.

But I had little reason to believe he considered my excessive gardening anything more than a diversion from an abusive husband.

"Name me one single solitary soul in all of the great state of Ohio who knows more about plants and planting than Emily Richards here does," Caitlin challenged as we swept into The Green Leaf.

Ira's steel-gray eyes and bemused face said he'd heard this charge before—more than once. He and I took it from there, and I was delighted to realize that a reputation of sorts had preceded me. In the course of our conversation, we touched on gardening with wildflowers and I suggested seeds and cuttings and root divisions, blue harebells and milkweed and dog-toothed violets. We worked through herb gardens, rosemary wreaths the ancient Greeks used to strengthen the memory, wintergreen poultices for boils and swelling, lavender plants for the production of top-notch honey.

I left the shop, inside of an hour, job in hand . . . if I wanted it. Embracing a rush of personal power I'd never felt before, I knew I had to make the most of it.

V
—

DESPITE MY DETERMINATION, I'D BEEN UNABLE TO confront Shane with my Wooster news and July passed without a decision. If August vanished too, Ira would surely drop his offer.

Shane was expected home from another weekend on the road, and so, while a grainy dove-gray Sunday dawned, I envisioned him in the bedroom doorway, icing the air with his rage. Fear threatened to squelch my tentative exhilaration. Still, I *had* to make a stand; the cycle had to be broken. This took far more courage than I had ever imagined.

The morning passed, plodding and oppressive. Sun-up sounds that normally lifted my spirits—the stir and scrap of crows, the whir of doves—all failed to rouse me, muffled as they were by the spotted rhythms of rain.

Neither Callum nor Kit stirred. I, too, lay in bed for hours, honing my lines. Well after ten, I dropped Datha's *Drift* CD into my nightstand player. One last chance to stand silver in the wind like blown glass.

Just before eleven o'clock, I woke Callum and Kit and outlined my plan. They were supportive and relieved and there were hugs and kisses all around, along with emphatic pronouncements about towing the line, bowing to authority, and so on, if only they would not be left behind, a thought that had not remotely occurred to me. Part of their euphoria, I suspected, sprang from a misguided belief that life without Shane meant fewer mown lawns. Nevertheless, their approval and acceptance were critical.

My own desperate hope, all my tenuous plans, the cautious optimism and burgeoning self-confidence, collapsed into a heap of rubble the moment Shane pulled the old Ford in out of the rain just after five o'clock.

Tired and disgruntled and reeking of alcohol, he raved—over several more beers—about a traffic snarl at the round-about on Elm Street, a cell phone call that had not been returned, a parking ticket from an Akron mall—he'd parked in a handicapped zone on his lunch break.

Showered and changed, he stepped outside to inspect the grounds. Though the rain had stopped, the sky kept its grim and threatening cast, and when he returned to the back porch, Callum's stubborn streak and Kit's girlish clumsiness gnawed on his blowsy spirit.

Out of habit, I dumped a bag of charcoal briquettes into the outdoor grill. The Richards always barbecued the Sunday Shane came in from weekend work. I knew this. Shane knew this. The neighbors knew this.

Shane lit the grill and sat down at the picnic table on the back deck.

If I didn't tell him now, I never would.

I reordered the mustard, the relish, the salt and paper shakers, the Worcestershire sauce, all in a neat and slim line at my end of the table. "Caitlin and I drove over to Wooster yesterday," I began.

Shane's eyes pinched shut.

"You know, over there to the nursery?" With only a shred of courage left, I rushed on. "I can have that job if I want it, Shane. Ira was so encouraging, and I'd really like to help out."

"Help out with what?" Shane's eyes popped open. "Haven't we beaten that horse to death already?"

The fire fizzled in the dampness, and Shane lurched to his feet. A second match flickered inches from my face, and when the flame singed Shane's fingers, he cursed and flicked it away.

"What did I tell you about that, Em?"

Barely audible now, Shane's words dropped around me

like acid. I retreated to the far side of the porch, but he swooped down on me like a bird of prey.

"I'll tell you what I see." His voice tightened, and his solid frame towered above me. "I see some stupid little girl who—just maybe—needs to be straightened out." With a glance left and right, he snatched my upper arm, tore open the back screen door, and hurled me inside.

I staggered across the room and slammed into the stove.

"You ungrateful little bitch," he hissed. "I keep you here in this fucking shithole like some goddamn queen. And what do I get for it? Shit. Nothing but shit." He reeled toward me as I slumped to the floor. "I told you to stay away from that bitch, didn't I? You think I make these things up just to hear myself talk? I said stay away, damn it. Or so help me God, I'll kill the both of you."

I pushed my back against the stove and tried to stand, my arms crooked over my head. But I could barely breathe now, and my body convulsed in terror.

Shane stepped back and laughed. And then, as I pushed myself halfway to my feet, my hands over my face, he hit me. One searing blow, left to right. From the metallic taste of blood, I knew that my lower lip had been split open. My eyes teared as the back of my head slammed against the refrigerator, and I clawed at the air for some support.

"Leave her alone, you bastard!" Callum's image wavered in the doorway. I caught the blur of him as I hit the floor.

"Goddamn mama's boy." Shane snatched the *Drift* disc from the tabletop where I'd left it. Two sharp blows bloodied my upper arm, and I screamed.

Weaving above me now, Shane sneered, and reaching for a fistful of hair, he wrenched me to my feet. Pinned by the throat against the refrigerator, fighting for air, I writhed under his weight. But his arm only tightened.

"Stop it, you fucking bastard!" Callum hurled himself

against his father's back, his fists pounding. Shane spun around and tossed the boy aside like a sack of flour. Callum hit the kitchen wall with a crackling thud and sank to the floor. With his booted foot, Shane slammed him in the stomach, and Callum howled with pain.

"My God, Shane," I whispered, my throat strangled and stiff. "He's your son. For God's sake. He's your own boy."

"Is he?"

Unable to stand under the oppressive heat of Shane's body, I crumpled to the floor again.

His arms twisted over his gut, Callum rocked on his knees, and behind him I could see Kit standing horror-stricken in the doorway.

God knows, I'd suffered before. But this—this rank and rancid pain—this was for my children. I would never let it stand.

I forced myself to my feet.

Shane's palsied black hulk stood panting and transfixed in the center of the room.

"Get up, Callum," I said, hobbling forward and helping Callum to his feet.

Shane collapsed into the nearest chair and propped his head in his hands.

"We're going to Caitlin's now," I said.

Her eyes raw with tears, Kit braced my battered body against her own, and with a quivering hand, she dabbed at the blood on my lips.

And then the three of us, together, straggled out the front door.

In the darkness we left behind, I could hear Shane's slurred plea. "I'm sorry, Em. You know I didn't mean it, Em. Em?"

Annie's Story

(In Her Own Words)

i

———

"TO ANNIE, WITH LOVE." I TRACE THE WORDS AS ROUND and bold as I can, so that the letters cover Raine's chest like globs of black oil. I took the original of this shot with my cell phone right here in Chicago at Datha's Walls for the Wind Tour concert at Midwest Telecom Arena eight years ago. I've had it taped over the bathroom mirror for a dog's age now, and it's cracked and curled like peeled paint. Still, since I can't bring myself to toss it out, I've hidden it away in one of Emma Stern's old hat boxes. The old bitty'll never know.

This new print is twice the size and sharper too. Something pure about it. I can brush the surface and the freshness seeps right in under my fingertips like spring air. Makes me smile.

I catch myself twisting a frizzle of hair around my forefinger, back and forth, back and forth. Bad habit, I know. The old bat rags on me all the time. "Your hair's gonna fall out like baby teeth," she says. I think she'd get off on that. Low-key love it, I mean.

Look at this picture. I can feel Raine's hand on my back, like a hot coal on my spine. He picked *me* out of the whole audience that night. We must have danced over the whole stage. Me and him, just me and him. I can smell the sweat and leather of him even now. And I gave him that ring he's wearing on his right hand, middle finger. A wine-red ruby in old gold.

"Annie. Annie, dear."

Damn wheedling old woman, leave me alone, for God's sake.

I scrunch up my shoulders. I scowl. I yank my shirt collar up around my ears. One more go at it.

Raine . . . there—looks something like old Victorian calligraphy. I know what his signature should look like. We all do. And this is it.

"Annie. Oh, Annie, dear."

That damn voice burns at the back of my throat like a lit match. I go back into the sitting room, but not before slipping the old nag's beaded change purse into a pocket of my poncho.

ii

⸺

ON A DIM LATE-APRIL MORNING I'M STILL UNDER THE covers twenty minutes past the rumble of Datha on my cell phone. I've lain here a jillion times, screwed up over whether or not to bother getting up at all. Who, beyond that sour old prig upstairs, would even notice?

But things have changed now. I'm this close to being free of fetching the morning paper for the old nag like some faithful lapdog.

My shitty single-room apartment in the basement of Mrs. Stern's Olive Street row-house rental has low walls that I've plastered with Datha posters. One window, high and hatch-like over the kitchen sink, lets in the scrappiest bit of sunlight. A wrought-iron fence outside leads up to the main entrance, where a wooden staircase inside climbs up to Emma's rat's nest on the second floor. Some sticks of furniture up there are still covered in bedsheets, so that the whole place looks like some gothic attic on moving day. The rest of the building is empty.

At seven thirty, I step out into the damp gloom of Chicago's morning sweat—greasy car exhaust and wet pavement. Red maples and black oaks march off down the street, and I slouch along beside them, behind a pair of black plastic sunglasses.

Twenty minutes and I'm at the corner of Olive and Chestnut. On the long daily slog over to Giorgio's for the old lady's newspaper, I always mean to give this place a miss. And there's not a day goes by that I don't blink. This red-brick Edwardian row house, with that shoebox garden out front, thumbs its nose at me—all those polished banisters, the marbled tiling, cut-glass chandeliers, silk-embroidered rugs. They suck me in like some spider's web. My throat slams shut with tears.

"Lovely old lady, isn't she?" Peppery hair sprouts from under the flowered head scarf of the old biddy beside me now. Her face is as plump and pink as an old sow's. "I'm new to the neighborhood," she says. "Not many of you young people appreciate such elegance these days. I do hope one of these lovely old things comes on the market soon."

"This one'll never be for sale," I tell her. "This is *Stern House*." I stab a finger at the brass plaque swinging over the front steps. "I'm moving back in with my mother at the end of the month. That's my room . . . there . . . on the top floor." I point to a stained-glass suncatcher bouncing in an open window on the third floor.

"Well, aren't you the lucky one."

It's been fifteen years come September that I last clamored up those stairs. If you asked me now, I'd say the old

Edwardian oozed class and care. But I can't think about it too long, or the ooze turns to rot. We all lived there together—me, my mother Maria, my grandmother Julia, her sister, old Emma Stern, and Emma's crotchety wino of a husband, Hubert—tripping over each other like barflies, buried under the polished silver, the stacks of bone china, the bare-ass hearths. And not much else. My mother and me were the Cinderellas of the piece, minus any sniff of a prince.

Emma Stern is my grandmother Julia's twin sister. Grandma was sicker than a lame poodle most of her life, starting right after she popped out, a good two minutes after Emma did. Least loved, she always said. That two minutes warped her mind big-time. And then decades of Julia-induced guilt brainwashed Emma and her smarmy CEO banker husband, Hubert, into throwing an obscene amount of their cash Julia's way, even taking in my mother, Grandma's out-of-wedlock rug rat. Seems their stuffy old Edwardian needed a housekeeper.

Julia, Maria, and me—Ma's very own bastard, no "daddy" in sight—we were all well stocked in the "things" department, so long as the treasure chest and the mothy consciences held out. But eventually, the Edwardian had to go. We adjusted. Emma crawled over to her present rental shabbiness, and me and Ma fell down into her basement, like rubbish in a bin.

"None of these will be sold for years." I sweep a hand from Chestnut down toward Beechnut. "My father owns the lot."

"How delightful. Life must be so exhilarating in such charming surroundings."

"Oh, yes."

Stern House choked us all with a mind-numbing stagnation. I'd had only vague acquaintances who'd lusted after the family's silver plate. Hubert would drag a scrawny finger along one tabletop or another, and say, "Surely this can't be your best work." And we'd dust till our knuckles bled.

In some small way I guess that must have eased the strain a string of operations for my bum leg put on the Stern purse strings. A "genetic deformity" was all anyone ever told me.

Hubert's portrait—those shitty John Lennon glasses, that steel-wool beard, and those cold, empty fish eyes—still ogles me from over the fireplace. One day I mean to smash it.

"The house we have now is beautiful in its own way," I say. "Lots of space. An Olympic-sized pool. And, of course, the guesthouse. But these old ladies have real character. It's all in what you get used to, I guess. Sometimes you just know where you belong."

"You're blessed to have such beauty in your life, young lady."

My throat has cramped up again, and I can only nod.

"Few people do, you know. Be good to the old place."

She pats my arm and moves off, and it's all I can do not to call her back. Instead, she fades away, and I'm back in silks and satins, standing at an open upstairs window—with Raine. (He pulled me into his arms that night and danced me across the stage.)

"You are the light." I'm startled by the sound of my own voice, and I grip Hubert's antique penknife in the pocket of my poncho. My eyes dart about like gnats, up the empty street and down again, before I can move on.

iii

—

"LISTEN UP MRS. STERN." I SHUTTLE THE OLD WOMAN'S wheelchair back from the curtained window, and those lashless piggy eyes blink at me like a ditzy owl as I sit down at the end of her bed. "Zip a lip, eh? Hubert's ring is gone. I mean *Gone Girl.*"

The old lady's bony knees, wrapped in that same ratty wine-colored kimono she always wears, well they knock up against me when I haul the chair forward, and her sickly face pitches in and out like some creepy rag doll. Her Q-tip hair's been thinning forever, and now wispy strands of it whip around at the back of her head like a halo. And she's put on that dying carp pout of hers too.

"I told you, the damn thing is gone. Don't know where. Don't know when."

Old Emma droops, and the wheelchair squawks like the rigging of an old ship. Jeez, I hate that sound. In fact, I despise every last living thing about the old fart and her digs —the stacked catalogs, all the unopened mail and half-filled grocery bags. Everything's gone as gamey as she has. I haul off and kick the front wheel of her chair, just missing her swollen right ankle, and she quivers like a plucked bowstring.

"Julia knows, Annie, dear. You ask your grandmother now. I gave Hubert that ring on our fortieth wedding anniversary." The eyes cloud up. "It was a ruby, for Hubert's birthday . . . in July. You will find it, won't you, Annie?"

I'm majorly ticked off now. "Stop it." I must be yelling. "Julia's been dead for over ten years now. Slipped on the damn ice downstairs the Christmas before Ma died."

We lock eyes, me and Emma Stern, and she finally looks away. But then her old lady face goes all sunny. "Your mother." She hooks a weedy finger right next to my cheekbone. "Maria will remember Hubert's ring. Ask your mother when she gets here. I don't know why she sent you over alone this morning. You're much too young for this kind of work. It's never done to Hubert's satisfaction as it is, much less with your inexperience. You know how careless you can be."

Emma's face goes all squishy then. "I know we don't get around like we used to, Julia and I," she says. "But everyone always says, 'Those Steinem girls are a handful.'" The bald eyes drift over to the curtained window. "Ask your mother now, Annie. Hubert will want that ring."

My face is all hot and twisted now. I jump up and limp across the room. "I'm twenty-eight years old, Mrs. Stern. I've taken care of you—on my own—for eight god-awful years. Before Ma died too. Me. Annie Brenner." I turn to face her and slap my chest with a fist. "Me. All alone. They're all dead but me. Now I want you to shut the hell up about that goddamn ring, once and for all."

"It was Hubert's, you see," Emma squeaks. She's tugging at the crinkles in that shredded housedress again. "A ruby . . . in old gold. He was born in July, you see. You will ask her, won't you, Annie?"

I'm counting to ten now. I don't want to have to give the old cow a smack upside the head. "Alright." I straighten up with a sniff. "I'll ask."

"That's my girl." Emma goes all bubbly-like and sinks back into her wheelchair. "Now where's the morning paper? The *Sun-Times* now, from Giorgio's. Not that awful rag . . ."

"Don't I always bring you the *Sun-Times*? Haven't I always. And don't I read you the whole damn thing . . . every morning . . . after breakfast?" I shuffle across to the room's floor-to-ceiling double-wide window and throw aside a blanket of musty red velvet drapes, raising a cloud of dust motes. Morning light slinks in through the sun-bleached lace underneath, and the room perks up a hair, though all the spring sunshine in Christendom could never stamp out the scent of old lady and decay.

There are times—not many—when I regret giving Raine

that ruby ring. Nothing from this crotchety old nag should ever touch him. But didn't he slip that ring on the same night? At least that's how I remember it anyway.

"Oh, now Annie, dear." Emma's voice jackhammers at the back of my head. "Your grandmother would blush to hear such language. But what does it say there about that young man of yours?"

I ratchet through the newspaper and settle back on the bed. "'Raine and Company Bring Real Rock 'n' Roll Back to Chicago,'" I read with righteous triumph from the bottom of the front page.

"Now in my day . . . " The old thing starts up and glances out the window. She stops, thank God, and turns back to me. "Well, that's that," she says, and shakes the cobwebs out of her head. "Did he take you dancing again?" Her eyes are glowing now, almost as brightly as mine must be. I skim the paper for Datha details.

"There was a sort of reception after the show," I tell her. "You know . . . backstage and all. Ah . . . here it is —'Raine, Datha's enigmatic lead singer'—blah, blah, blah"— (I have to wing it here)— "with his long-time companion, Anne Brenner, from the city. Oh . . . and look here." I swoosh the paper under Emma's nose. "Here he is . . . on-stage at the MTA. Quite an eyeful, eh?"

Emma hasn't begun to focus when I snatch the paper away. Raine's hands are cupping the top of his microphone stand, Hubert Stern's ring on an index finger.

"Well, let me see the fellow, at least," Emma whines.

"It's a poor shot, really." I squint. Can that really be Hubert's ring? Was it really so small? "The printing's off-kilter," I say. "It's all a big blur. With your eyes, you'd never make out a thing." I'm up and back at the lace curtains, my face to the window. I work the photograph from the paper and slip it under a potted geranium on the sill.

"Here." I round the foot of the bed, take up a white plastic bottle marked *DIGITALIS* from Emma's nightstand, and drop two small sleeping pills into her outstretched hand. "Take your meds now. We'll finish the paper later."

"You will bring him by sometime, won't you, Annie?"

I shove the wheelchair closer to the bed.

"You've promised so often. It's so tiresome here day after day. All alone. No one to visit with. No one to talk to."

(*What am I? Chopped liver?*)

"Not that I'm complaining"

(*The hell you aren't.*)

"You know how grateful I am."

(*No. Not really.*)

I settle the old thing on the covers and drape a soiled patchwork quilt over her thinness.

"He'll be by sometime soon. I promise. Take your meds now and rest." I pass her a tumbler of water and wait until the pills are gone. When I leave the room, the newspaper and Hubert's antique pocket watch—the very last thing of any value on Emma's dressing table—leave with me.

iv

I SHRUG OFF THE PAIN IN MY RIGHT LEG AND MOVE across Olive Street, walking east, just under a mile, to the metro station on Huntington. Overcrowded buses and overcrowded Loop trains sweep me through morning rush hour, deep into the idle, sterile lives of the South Side.

"You got some change, lady?" I'd seen this kid coming from the back of the bus.

"Sorry," I say. "I've got just enough here to get me over to my grandfather's house with a bit of homemade soup." I pat the puffed-up lap of my poncho. "He hasn't eaten since the day before yesterday."

The kid sniggers and curls his lip, but he backs off, and when the old man beside me sneezes into the back of his hand, I have to cover my mouth and nose with a fist.

At the E Street Station, I get off and head over to the pawnshop on the next corner, half a block away. *LEON'S* flashes in ice-blue globs above a drunk sprawled in the doorway. I pull a Datha scarf tight about my face and step inside.

LEON'S is long and narrow, cramped with magazines, packaged food, liquor, and cigarettes, all running off in rusting racks along the walls. The center aisle's low, open shelving holds a hodgepodge of ticketed items. Cigar smoke swills under the harsh ceiling lights.

Behind a Formica counter at the back of the room, Leon, a flat-faced man with spiky red hair and an ugly purple mole on his cheek, watches me with dull gray eyes. He's slumped over the countertop, his waxy forearms spreading out on the cracked surface like lard. His stubby hands are working over something that flashes in the folds of a rag he's pulled pretty close to his chest. The room reeks of stale sweat, cigar smoke, and urine.

"Back already?" Leon wheels a stogie side to side in his mouth. "So whatcha got now, little lady?" He plops the rag on the countertop with a dull thud. "Couldn't get jack shit for that goddamn switchblade you hauled in here the other day. Same for the pocketbook. Fuckin' beads." He jerks the cigar from his mouth, coughs once, and spits on the floor behind him. "Some fuckin' whore down on Michigan Avenue's got an eye out for that kind of shit. Beads, bangles, baubles. You name it. What you got for me now?"

I hug the scarf to my neck and pull out Hubert Stern's pocket watch. "It was my great-grandfather's," I say, laying the watch on the countertop. "He was a wealthy German businessman. Came over from Saxony in the 1880s. Eloped with the family maid, or so they say." I snicker. "I had it appraised once. It's worth quite a lot." (Just a little more cash, and I'll be set.)

"Came over from Germany, did he?" Leon's eyes go all small and piggy. "Wealthy, huh?" He stands up, fixes a hand to either side of the watch, and wags his head side to side like an old dog on a bone. "I'll give you thirty bucks for the damn piece. Best I can do. I ain't got much of a market for this kind of shit. Now you bring me a Colt carbine, little lady, and we're in business." He laughs again, a dead sound that ends in a spasm of coughs.

"That's okay." I swallow hard and wet my lips. "Thirty's okay."

Leon wheezes, lumbers over to the cash register, and pops the bottom drawer open with a flat slap against the palm of his hand.

Outside the shop, the drunken sot has pulled himself upright and begins to urinate against the front window. Leon curses, drops a few bills on the countertop, and heads for the door.

Left behind, I stuff the rag and its contents, the watch, the money—and a fistful more from the open till—into the pockets of my poncho.

Leon has slimed himself through the front door and stands flailing his arms over the lush's bent head. Right behind him, I grab two bags of tortilla chips from a display rack and cram them into another pocket, and while Leon's cursing blends with the yelps from the old drunk, I scramble off down the street.

I'm moving faster than I have in years. I make my bus, and just as Leon's bulk rolls into the E Street Station, we pull away.

I snap open a bag of chips and munch in silence for a

good half hour. Whatever Leon has in that grimy rag—and I've had a bad feeling about that since I ripped it off—well, it punches against my thigh like a hammer.

On my last transfer I can't ignore the weight of it any longer. I'm the only passenger now, so I haul the thing up and sneak a peek.

"Good God!" I whisper, and shove the horror out of sight.

Annie's got a gun.

V
—

"SO, HOW'S IT GOING, ANNIE, MY GIRL?" GIORGIO Zafarelli braces himself over the back counter of his shop on thick, stubby arms. Black eyes in a round and balding face meet mine as I close the door with a muffled whir.

"Okay, I guess."

"A little late this morning, aren't we?" Giorgio slips a *Sun-Times* from a stack beside the cash register, folds it once, and slides it across the counter as I step up. "Old lady Stern'll have you for breakfast, you being so late again."

"She can wait," I say. "It's not like she's going anywhere."

I love this corner store—*ZAFARELLI'S* in bright red paint over the door, the deli smells, Italian foods boxed and bottled and canned.

Ever since my mother's suicide—an event no one has mentioned for years now—*ZAFARELLI'S* has been the only place she's the least bit real to me anymore. I love the way the sunlight fires up the cherrywood floors. I love the way the screen door opens with a soft whine and snaps shut again, rebounding—just once—like a loose spring. There's something as powerful about the place to me as Stern House.

I plop two Rolos on top of the newspaper. "Don't say it,

Mr. Z. Mrs. Stern yaks it up all day long about diets. Mama did too, remember? Like it had something to do with legs."

Giorgio taps a plump finger on the back of my hand. "Your ma always felt bad for you comin' into this world with this leg trouble." He punches the register open. "Why she'd go on and on day to day, fretting about what she must have done wrong. What she should have done different. Like it was her fault, you see. But that kind of thing just happens, you know." He pauses and clears his throat. "Like I've said before, I got this cousin over there in the Big Apple. Big man. Like an elephant, you know. He's gotta have them special shoes made, one heel three, maybe four inches higher than the other? That kind of thing just happens. Ain't nobody's fault." He crosses his arms on his chest and rocks forward. "Been botherin' you this morning, has it?"

"A bit." I shift my weight, pull my purse from the poncho, and lay it on the countertop.

"Old lady's check again, eh?" The till rings open, and I pass over Mrs. Stern's Social Security check. "How's the old lady keeping these days? Barrel of laughs like always, I expect." Giorgio counts the money onto the countertop. "Fifty. One hundred. One fifty, Two hundred. Two fifty. Three hundred." He slips the bills into an envelope, which he hands to me. "I remember years ago . . . she used to come in here herself. Like she owned the place. The high and the mighty Emma Stern. Thought she was the cat's ass. And always after my Sophie. Fetch this. Fetch that. I figure that's how come my Sophie took off back East when she did. I might get a word, maybe two from her nowadays." His voice cracks here, and he sucks in his breath. "You'd best get on over there, Annie, or she'll set the cops on you."

"No hurry." I wrap the envelope with a rubber band. Envelope into purse, purse into poncho. "See you tomorrow, Mr. Z."

Giorgio nods and smiles as I back away toward the door. He spreads a newspaper out under his arms and glances down at the front page. "You betcha, Annie, my girl," he says. "Tomorrow then."

I make my way down past the deli case, and, at the shelf nearest the front door, I reach into a canister and come up with a handful of pepperoni sticks. I stash these in an empty pocket. Giorgio might notice. Giorgio might not. I can't say. He keeps his head down, his eyes glued on his paper. But I don't much care anymore what anybody sees.

vi
—

"I'LL JUST BE GONE THE WEEK. THERE SHOULDN'T BE any problems," I say to the woman at the desk. She drums her fingers on her coffee mug, and I drag my chair closer.

The small white cubicle where we sit is packed with file cabinets and sagging shelves. Warning lists and other lame advice layer the bulletin boards tacked up on the walls. My nerves jangle. I can't possibly stay here much longer.

"This is Emma Stern from Olive Street?" The woman sits back and readjusts a pearly pin at the back of her head, where netting holds her gray hair in a tight bun.

I nod.

The woman rifles through a stack of files to her left, fishes out a thin one from near the bottom, and scowls. "*Emma Winetta Stern*," she reads. "Ah, yes. Lucy took your call this morning." Her sharp face bends over a sheaf of paper taken from the file, and then her pukey brown eyes pin me down over the top of her glasses. She gives me a half-hearted smile. "And you are?"

"Annie Brenner." I shift in my seat. "I'm Mrs. Stern's

niece." My eyes fasten on the woman's folded hands, and I motion to the door behind me. "Like I told the girl outside, I have to go to Buffalo for my sister's wedding. I hate to leave the poor thing on such short notice, but it can't be helped. I've used you people before."

"Yes . . . yes. It's all here." The woman's forehead crinkles, and she purses her prissy red lips. "You have Mrs. Stern's medications in hand, I assume?" She looks up. "We don't take on any of that responsibility. We're solely home-care companions."

"We're all set there," I tell her. "Mrs. Stern's such a sweet old thing." I laugh—a twitter of sound that feels forced even to me. "I've always made sure she's had the best of care."

The old bitty drops her eyeglasses on the closed file, laces her fingers on top, and taps her thumbs together. A scream pushes up from my gut and tickles the back of my throat, but I cram it back down.

The woman stands up—at last. "We'll have someone come by the middle of next week to get acquainted with Mrs. Stern's schedule," she says. "But I don't anticipate any problems, provided you have adequate facilities for a resident stay."

Oh . . . thank God.

Thank God. Thank God.

It's all settled then. Home Health Care Advocates will see to Mrs. Stern while I'm gone. We shake hands over the desktop, and with a flick of her wrist and a crisp "all done then," the woman dismisses me.

vii
—

LATE JULY AND THE CHICAGO SKY HUNKERS LOW AND black in a damp breeze slinking in from the lake as I set off on the last of my preflight arrangements. For years now, prescriptions for this Digitalis—something to do with Mrs. Stern's heart—have followed on one outpatient clinical visit or another. I've always pried out a written order. None of that electronic shit. How do I know where I'll be able to fill it? I've always ignored the specifics too. Medications can be stretched to one or two pills a week, increased whenever the old lady crabs about this ache or that pain. She gets on just as well with aspirin and sleeping pills. And the money I've saved! Co-pays aren't cheap, you know.

I head over to the pharmacy on Indian Grove. It's a long hike, but the pharmacist there, a geeky East Indian with thick black-rimmed glasses and a bow tie, never remembers me. Never asks any stupid questions.

As I near the shop, I skim the familiar slip of paper. A February date has become a July one. A little inky emphasis on the first two strokes of a two and there it is—a seven. I've done it before. I'll do it again. A one to a five. A seven to a nine. A three to an eight.

With everything I've taken from the old lady's Social Security checks—minus the very minimum in living expenses—and the bits and pieces I've pried out of Leon for Emma's doodads, well . . . I've finally accumulated enough money to fly off to Raine in Scotland the first week in August.

In a day or two, I'll print out my boarding passes.

viii
—

EDINBURGH, DARK AND GOTHIC, LIES OUTSIDE MY OPEN
window, smelling of wet stone and car exhaust. I kick off my
shoes and sprawl on the bed of a B&B in a terraced Victorian
brownstone on Coates Gardens near the West End. I've been
up twenty-four hours now. Late yesterday afternoon to
O'Hare by taxi for the long haul to Gatwick, and then north
on British Rail—four hours plus—to Waverley Station.

Now and then, my mind throws up Emma's grim face in
the Edwardian's upstairs window as my cab pulled away.
Worn and annoyed, she'd crabbed and crabbed about "ne-
glect" and "desertion." What a treat to be rid of the tired
old thing. The teenage girl the agency sent over just shook
her head. Too many old nags in her life, too, I guess.

From the patchy fields north of London, through all the
greens of the countryside, the cluttered towns and soggy
Scottish Lowlands, the sky has held a chalky whiteness. But
now, end-of-day August sunlight creeps across the high plastered ceiling of my room and crawls down the opposite wall.

Raine is out there . . . somewhere. Breathing the same
Scottish air. Watching the same close of the same day. I
ache to go to him, but I can barely move. My eyes shut on
everything but the shadow of his face, and I sleep the
dreamless sleep of exhaustion.

ix
—

EIGHT A.M. A WATERY SUN POKES AROUND THE ROOM, AND
Edinburgh lurches back to life with fizzling traffic in rain-
soaked streets and the groan of a sea wind at the window.

With heavy eyes, I trace the patterns on the room's greenish-gold wallpaper—ribbons and rosebuds, small birds and shafts of wheat. A roll of nerves spirals through my chest.

I get up and wash at the porcelain sink, cold air raising a shiver. Over the same clothes I've worn from Chicago—tan-colored slacks and a frothy pea-green blouse—I yank on my poncho, fastening it at the neckline with a favorite sterling-silver Datha broach. I'm as close to Raine as I've been since our onstage dance.

After breakfast, my B&B hostess drones on with endless directions to Duddingston village. A main bus east down Haymarket Terrace to Princes Street and the city center. A second bus down Dalkeith Road, east, past Arthur's Seat, to Duddingston on its tiny loch. Ravenhill, the band's recording studio and management office, is on Old Church Lane, within walking distance of the Duddingston Station.

I reach the heart of the city in under an hour. Snarling traffic and gobs of pedestrians make a mess of my early morning hopefulness. Of all places, Raine's hometown should be special. I press my back against the cold wet stone of the Bank of Scotland and blink at the passing crowd. Rat-faced businessmen in flapping trench coats carrying enormous black umbrellas. School girls barking like pods of seals. Window-shoppers and gawking tourists.

My eyes pinched shut, I clamp my hands over my ears and raise my head to a spray of clean rain. The blank sky that smothers the city has smoothed the high Gothic curves of terraces and Victorian squares. The city shows me all of its romantic possibility. Still enough goodness here for Raine, I think, and pulling my collar up against a rising wind, I head for my Duddingston connection.

By the time I step off my last bus in a light drizzle, the air has sharpened to a razor's edge.

I reach the studio in under five minutes. From magazine

clippings and fanzine reading, I spot the building right off—an old Georgian on a grassy rise, behind a high black metal fence. In the cold and rain, three bay windows across the ground floor are cozy with lamplight. Upper floors blaze through the twisted limbs of oak trees.

RAVENHILL in wrought iron marks the right-hand side of an open gate. I trace each letter with numbing fingers, pitch up the hood of my poncho, and start up the hill. The paved driveway sweeps in an arched curve from street-level past the building at the top of the hill, and then drops down again further up Old Church Lane.

In sunlight, the place must gleam like sea salt. But in this dripping gloom, the building melts into mist at either end, and I'm a bit spooked. My leg aches too. Inside the gate, I stop to catch my breath and glance up.

Just then, the room over the main entrance goes dark. Someone is standing there. I know it. Raine. It must be Raine. And didn't that shadow shift? There. Wasn't that a wave? My fingers are stiff with the cold, but I reach up and rain dribbles down my sleeve. I wait until the shadow disappears, and then I pull my arm back in and head for the marble steps that lead to the front door.

Inside the vestibule, a chandelier speckles the inside walls like candles in a sanctuary. The massive oak door closes behind me with a thud, and I slip out of my poncho, shake it once over the tiled floor, and sling it up on a hook to the right of a second, smaller door with a long, glazed window. A paisley scarf in green and black and scarlet pokes out from the sleeve of the men's black leather jacket next to my poncho. Green and black and red. Isn't that the same scarf Raine drapes around his neck in the band's new "Speaking Eyes" video? I throw my poncho back on and cram the scarf into an empty pocket. When I open the inner door, a small bell jangles overhead.

The large room I've entered is homey and wood-paneled. An open fireplace blazes to the left. Three overstuffed black leather chairs are pulled up to the heat there. Several others face a rain-washed bay window beside the fireplace. Near the back of the room, a hallway moves off to another wing of the building. To my right, a wide cream-colored marble staircase curls up to the upper floors and down into the basement. A low rumble drifts up from the studio below.

He *is* here. My breath sharpens.

Directly in front of me stands a broad oak desk, the walls behind lined with built-in ivory-colored bookshelves. I can just see the end of a conference table and a scatter of chairs through an open doorway behind the desk, floor-to-ceiling windows looking out on a rain-washed garden.

The smell of burning cedar fills the room, and I breathe this in like incense. In a heartbeat then, I rush forward, give the desk the once-over, and stash away two black fountain pens, a packet of masthead envelopes, and a small rubber stamp, each marked with *RAVENHILL* in gold lettering.

I hurry back to the door just as a nasty-looking woman in a gray double-breasted power suit appears in the doorway of the conference room. The woman closes a spiral notebook and with over-bright eyes traces my footprints door to desk and back. She smirks and drops a pair of eyeglasses onto her chest, where they dangle from a fine black chain. "May I help you?" she asks with a light Irish lilt as she moves behind the desk.

"Yes, you can. I'm Annie Brenner. I'm here to see Raine."

"Ah, to be sure." The woman smiles again.

"No, really." I brush the desktop with fingertips so firm I could be eradicating some stain. "I'm sure he already knows I'm here. If you could just tell him, I know he'll see me."

The woman clears her throat and sits down. "I'm sorry, love, but Raine isn't available just now."

Over a long, frazzled breath, I squint at the ceiling. "I'm Annie Brenner," I tell her again. "Annie Brenner? From Chicago? He'll be available for me. If you'll just run along now and tell him that I'm here."

The old lady's face hardens. "I am sorry, my dear," she grouses, her eyes flashing. "Miss Brenner, is it?"

"Yes, Annie Brenner. From Chicago."

"I'm sorry, Miss Brenner. But I'm afraid none of the lads are able to see you at all this morning."

"Raine will. If you just tell him I'm here, damn it. I know he'll see me."

The woman stands up. "I'm afraid you don't understand," she says. "They're all very busy."

I'm fidgeting with my hair now and fingering a short silver letter opener—a miniature dirk, really—that's lying on the desk. "He *will* see me," I say. "You just have to be a smidgen more chipper and let him know that I'm here. Do you think you can do that?"

The woman has taken a half step back from the desk. But she gives me another smarmy grin. "Why don't you have a seat, Miss Brenner. By the fire. You'll be more comfortable there, to be sure. I'll be right back."

I back away toward the fireplace. "Tell him Annie's here," I say, as the woman vanishes down the hallway to my right. "Annie Brenner. From Chicago. He'll know." Several long seconds pass before I dash back and snag the letter opener.

My pulse throbbing in anticipation, I sink into a chair by the fireplace and close my eyes. Shadows shift like dancers behind my eyelids. (The warmth of his hand in the small of my back. The scent of leather and sweat.) When I look up again, *he*'ll be there.

Footsteps. Two people. One slight and small. One firm and rhythmic.

I push up from the chair, turning as I stand, step forward, and open my eyes.

"Who the hell is he?" I grope for the dirk and cup the handle in the palm of my hand as I slump against the back of the chair.

The old hag is planted there again, beside a chunky dark-eyed man in a navy-blue uniform, "Security" stitched in gold on the left shoulder.

"So you'll be wanting to see Raine, then, are you now, lassie?" The man flashes his puppet's teeth under a coal-black moustache.

"You little bitch." I glare at the woman.

Her arms crossed and her lips tight, she stares back.

"You didn't tell him, did you?"

"Good life, now, lassie," the man says. "Why the lad's not to be bothered, don't you see? That's the way of it. Now if it's a line or two you'd be wanting to say to him, why Mrs. Burke here will see to it as the lad has it."

I pull myself up as straight and tall as I can. "There's no message." I turn around and plunk back down in my chair. Twenty minutes past eleven the clock on the fireplace mantle says. "I'll just wait right here," I say. "Until I *can* see him."

This announcement must have blown them away. I can hear them muttering behind my back as I count the up-turned bars on the fireplace grate. Eleven—twelve. One—two—three.

"Good life, lassie. That you will not." The security guard has stepped over. "It's galey weather, it is, but you'll be off now." He motions me from my chair. "The lads will not be up for some time. And by the set of your mind as it is now, you'll not be here when they do, as I'm standing here." He reaches for my arm.

"Keep your goddamned hands off me." I spring to my feet and limp over to the window, where he follows.

"That's enough now, lassie." The man's face is all knots now. "We keep our doors open here. But not for such as yourself. And I doubt we'll be after changing our minds. So you'll be off now. By your power or by mine."

Tears have boiled up into my eyes. This is how he lives now? With this hostility? The mean spirits? The empty souls?

"I won't go." I push my back against the windowpane, and the cold sears my shoulders. Under my poncho, I clench the dirk. "Tell him I'm here." I'm shouting now. "Just tell him I'm here, damn it! He *will* see me. I know he will."

Mrs. Burke has dropped out of sight. I can hear her mumbling to herself somewhere off to my right, behind the bulk of the security guard.

"Trouble, Colin?"

My eyes graze Colin's shoulder.

Mrs. Burke is standing there again. But it's *him* I see.

Magnificent. Slim and solid. In black jeans. Black boots. Black T-shirt. He has a hand on Mrs. Burke's arm. But he's looking straight at *me*. I can barely breathe.

"And you must be . . . Annie?" Raine glances at Mrs. Burke, who nods.

He's remembered. Of course, he'd remember.

Colin steps aside.

"Yes. Annie Brenner. From Chicago. In the United States."

Raine folds his arms on his chest. The ring on his left hand clouds and shrivels in the shallow light from the window. The setting is pale silver, almost glassy, with not a speck of ruby red. It might be some other ring altogether.

"I don't think it's a good idea for you to be here right now, Annie," Raine says, and I'm drowning in the sweetness of his voice.

"And I don't think you should come here again."

Some other place then? Some other time?

"I just had to see you again," I whisper.

"And so you have. But I think you should leave now."

He reaches for me. I take his hand and we disappear . . . together . . . enwrapped . . . sheltered by an inexhaustible primordial energy. Something beyond words, beyond time . . . at least until he says *goodbye*.

And then I glide outside, transfixed, and stand there in the rain for over an hour.

X

I HAVE TO LEAVE FOR GATWICK IN THE MORNING.

One full day of travel, the studio and offices on Monday, and then three more days in Duddingston outside Raine's home. Home should have come first. I know that now. But it's too late for regrets.

For the first time since my arrival, Edinburgh's skies clear to a patchy blue, like smudges on a canvas. The city rolls out in front of me, Castle Rock rearing up in gray granite, Georgian terraces spreading out their flowered squares at its base.

I leave the B&B early, and a now familiar maroon-colored bus brings me to the Duddingston station, from where I walk to Raine's home.

Yesterday, and the day before, and the day before that, I waited outside the gate for over four hours. No one came and no one went. Not even any other Datha fans.

In the sunlight, through the bars of a locked gate, across the lawn, an imposing Georgian facade rises up in pale gold, stone steps curving up to the front door.

Gray-stone cottages, fronted with summer flowers, line

the narrow lane opposite the mansion. At one of these, behind a mossy rock wall, an old white-haired woman in a
flowered blue dress and woolen shawl is working over a
clump of rosebushes as painfully crimson as Raine's scarf
now around my neck. Snipping away with small silver clippers, the old lady tosses her cuttings to the ground.

I saunter over. "Excuse me," I say. "Do you know the
man who lives in that house?"

"Oh, aye," she says. "And a good morning to you, lassie."
She straightens and brushes the hair from her wrinkled face.
"And a bonnie lad he is, too, that one."

I pinch one of the satin petals between my fingers. "He's
a good friend of mine, you know, and we've somehow just
missed each other." The woman's smile creeps right up into
her eyes. "I suppose a lot of people stop by here to see him."

"Oh, aye. That they do now. Especially the young lassies
such as yourself. A bonnie lad, that one. But he's off for the
continent now, don't you know."

My heart falls to pieces right then and there, and I can
hardly speak.

The woman cups one of the bright buds in her hand.
"Whenever he's about the place, he stops by for a wee bud
from the garden. And it's a rose he'll have so long as I've a
rose to give. It was one of these he took with him, late last
night."

The rose head glows like a live coal in the palm of her
hand.

He's gone? How can that be? There must be some mis-
take.

"Are you sure?" I ask. "I mean, did you *see* him leave?"

"Oh, aye. Quite sure I am of it now, I'm sorry to say. He
was by, as I say, late last night. Something quite sudden, so
he says. He'll be back again in a fortnight."

I swallow hard and force a smile, sad and sorry that

things have come to this for him. Locked in with those wretches at the studio. But I have no choice now but to let him go.

I turn to leave, and some small salvation springs to mind. "Could I have one of your roses, do you think? It's amazing really. But whenever we see each other, he brings me a rose just like this one. It's something very special between us. I've always wondered where they came from."

"It's a great idea some people have." With another deep smile, the woman hands me one perfect unblemished blood-red rosebud. "And now you'll have the same wee blossom as the lad himself. He left with one just here." She taps her temple. "In the band of his cap."

I close my eyes and drink in the sweetness. And then my eyes pop open again. "I know this will sound mad," I say. "But could I get a selfie of the two of us? On my cell phone here? It would mean a lot to me. I could send you a copy when I get back home."

"Oh, aye, to be sure."

The old woman trundles off across the lane on my arm. I arrange her in front of Raine's gate and slip in beside her. We lock arms, and holding the phone at arm's length, I tap the screen.

And that's exactly how I got this snap of Raine's Scottish housekeeper, Maggie. After a cup of tea, she showed me around the house. I spent some time alone with Raine, and when I left, he gave me this rose for remembrance.

He may never be truly safe and whole in this place, with Colin and that hideous Mrs. Burke to deal with. But I'll think about all of that later.

Dana's Story

i

THE MAN ASLEEP ON MY BED HAS LONG DARK HAIR in a wild sprawl down his back. On the smooth plane of his left shoulder blade, a mottled bluish tattoo reads *Scotland Forever*. Datha has sloughed off the night, and the music now dallies in the room like a bored and impatient houseguest.

From the final flash of day, you stood silver in the wind, like blown glass.

The man asleep on my bed has exhausted himself in my body, a memory now cloaked in tangled sheets and the scent of stale sex. Sitting at the open window of my first-floor San Diego apartment, I crush a cigarette in an over-filled ashtray and study the man.

In the predawn graininess, the pale, angular face I'd once seen there—Raine's—the faint outward jut of the jaw, the deep-set blue-green eyes, all dissolve like so much sea salt.

Such times are over and gone, crying for the light. A crimson rose in a dead plain.

This man is leaner than Raine. Raw-boned and weedy, his chest tanned and sleek. He has long, slim fingers, where Raine's are solid and comforting. In fact, so little about this man resembles Raine at all, beyond the glistening black hair and a gentle Gaelic accent, that when he comes around and speaks to me, I can only answer with a faint smile. And so he leaves, as so many others have done before him.

I tap out another cigarette, my eyes scanning the city—daybreak, a rising swell of early morning traffic, salted spring winds perfumed with sugar bush and rosebud. A hard copy of the spring edition of *Conversations* lies curled up under my left thigh. I finger this absentmindedly, cigarette smoke feathering the air.

Datha's music creeps around the room on pinpricks, Raine's voice a steady sweetness that my thoughts trail behind like streamers.

You stand in my vacant eye. All that is.

ii

——

THERE'S ANOTHER MAN IN MY ROOM. A MAN WITH coarse black hair dusted in the soft light that spills in through my bedroom window. He's heavyset about the neck and shoulders and speaks with a light Irish brogue, contrived but not unpleasant. Sex with this man will be something soft and fluid, not merely physical.

"This is smart stuff, Dana. Inventive . . . inspired." Sherika Stanhope thumbs through the manual—*Risk and Empowerment*—I've shared with her over lunch.

The man in my bed fades to black, and I'm ushered back into the present.

"The district is really buzzing, girl. Positive feedback, top to bottom. Such a unique take on juvenile substance abuse. Encourages kids to take some responsibility for themselves. Be a player. Time and energy are two things high school teachers rarely have enough of, and yet you can still churn out something like this." She taps the booklet with a ruby-red fingernail.

I nod as the waitress slips a lunch ticket to the center of the table.

"So—" Sherika slaps the tract with the back of her hand. "Michael Allyn? Homicide? San Diego's finest . . . and that's a personal observation, I might add. He's volunteered to help implement the program as it works itself out over the summer." Sherika picks up the bill. "Wants to hook up. Talk specifics?"

I nudge aside my half-eaten club sandwich and Sherika's umber eyes flash in her dusky face.

"Get it together, girl," she says. "I checked out that crowd top of the hour. CEOs. Corporate lawyers. Insurance thugs on a slum lunch."

I wave aside the foursome in pinstripes in the booth to Sherika's back.

"What . . . a man in the room and Dana Morrison hasn't had him weighed and measured yet?" She leans forward and throws up her hands. "Where have you been, girl? Fixated on that bozo you picked up at O'Connell's last weekend?"

"He wasn't a bozo," I say, reconciled at last to the present. "Well . . . not entirely."

"The hell he wasn't. What would you call, 'Top of the mornin' to ya, sugar' at ten p.m.? And I've heard a better Irish accent from my East LA gran. You know what I'm sayin'?"

"Ah . . . but he was a cute little thing. Those big blue eyes. All that long, loose dark hair. Cute. In a desperate, pleading sort of way." I snatch the check from Sherika's outstretched hand. "What can I say? It was a rough week. *I* was desperate. But *he* was pleading. At least I sent him home with a big smile and a pack of day-glow condoms."

"Whatever." Sherika rummages in her purse and hands over two twenty-dollar bills. "My treat," she says. "Anyway . . . Michael Allyn? SDPD? I said you'd probably be at O'Connell's if he shows up some weekend."

"Yeah. Sure. Why not. The more the merrier." I check my watch and give the foursome a parting scan. "Even with spring semester winding down, those afternoon classes aren't going to start without us, are they?"

"Better hit the road then," Sherika says, jumping to her feet.

iii

—

"FELICIA'S PASSÉ THEN, IS SHE?"

Behind his thick glasses, Ethan winces. The young woman in animated conversation across the room with our father has already mesmerized several members of Ethan's accounting firm.

"I must say, she's taking it rather well." The rigor with which Ethan swirls the ice in his tumbler tells me everything. "Oh, come on now, big brother. We're talking divorce here, not some highfalutin' corporate grandstanding. You've told *me*, and you haven't told *her*? She should read the proceedings in the society pages? And what's she done, exactly? Birthday cake not up to snuff? Jason not cracking *Othello* now that he's all of eight?"

We sip our gin and tonics in silence, and I watch as Felicia, inclining toward our father, bubbles out something that clearly charms every man within earshot. Tall, slender, and elegant, in a satin sheath matched to her sea-green eyes, she's a beauty. No doubt about it.

"And you have no regrets at all about this do you?" I ask Ethan.

"Irreconcilable differences," he intones, and drains his glass.

I tap the ashes from my cigarette into the potted schefflera beside me. "That would be Dad's excuse. He's the lawyer. You're the stodgy homebody tax consultant. More the bottom-line type."

"Maybe it is the bottom line," Ethan offers after some reflection, and clinks the ice in his emptied glass. "She has no sense of priorities. I don't know where the money goes."

"This is about money?" I'm genuinely shocked. "Where do you think the money goes? She's an ex-model, for God's sake. It's on her back. It's in her face. But you knew that when you married her. There's another woman, isn't there?" I don't wait for Ethan's reply. "Women split when they can't take it anymore," I say. "Men only leave if they've got somewhere else to go."

We twirl our cocktail sticks through another lengthy silence.

"She deserves more than an open door and a 'ciao, baby,' don't you think?" I pull up another cigarette from my clutch bag and light up. "Why is it that all of your women end up in the debit column? That's not very fiscally responsible, is it?"

"There's no one else," Ethan says, and I know he's lying. But he clears his throat and gives me nothing more.

"So . . .wife number three bites the dust." I clink my glass to Ethan's. "Felicia was everything you wanted, remember? Beauty. Charm. A bit on the vacant side, to be honest. But you knew that too. You demand so much, big brother. And then when you get it all, you toss it out like stale bread, like so much used furniture."

"Isn't that the pot and kettle thing?" Ethan grins and rolls his eyes, and I know I deserved that. "Plenty of moldy rolls stacked up around your digs. And you've shuffled around more odds and ends than half a dozen moving companies."

I swipe at Ethan's arm. "I know, I know. Mr. Wrong tails me like a drunk at an Irish wake." I wink over the rim of my drink. "But I've never married him."

"Touché." Ethan raises his glass. "A few close calls though, if memory serves."

"Far too many and far too close."

"Remember Joey Jessop?"

"How could I forget—much as I've tried."

"What were you, twenty-two? Twenty-three? Moved in with him until the day he knocked you across the room with the back of his hand. We pulled you out the very next day. And what about Sean what's-his-name?"

"You mean mother's Irish delusion?"

Her ears must have been burning because just then, my mother, Eleanor Morrison, erect and confident, her graying rust-red hair encircling a pale, still youthful face, drifts by on one of her maternal rounds.

"And a very happy birthday to you, dear." She squeezes Ethan's arm and kisses his cheek. "Such a lovely party. Felicia is just a natural at this sort of thing, isn't she?"

"Not for long," I say.

My mother appears not to register this remark. Instead she turns her large green eyes on me. "No beau this evening?" she says. "Whatever happened to Sean? From Ethan's wedding?"

My brother and I trade cynical smiles. I've yet to tell either of them that at the time of Ethan's first marriage, Sean had been likewise spoken for—a circumstance he'd neglected to share with me. I had just turned twenty-one. His was the first in a long line of similar such betrayals that had tainted my vision and left me a "spinster" far past my mother's notion of a sell-by date. Lost but not forgotten, Sean remains a celestial dance in her Irish eyes.

"Fifteen years ago now, Mother. Ethan's *first* go at marital bliss, remember?" I pass my brother a withering glance.

"I know, dear. But he was such a fine-looking young fel-

low. Well established, too, in that prestigious LA law firm—
Faulkner, Walker, Walker, something, something."

"It was the thighs, Mother. Don't you remember?
'Watch those thighs,' you used to say. 'All the boys will.'"

"Oh . . . I never meant anything by that, dear."

"It doesn't matter anymore." I give her hand a light
squeeze.

"And is someone watching *now*?"

Ethan coughs and fingers the ice in his glass. "Shall I
count the ways?"

iv

AS THE HIGH SCHOOL YEAR COMES TO A CLOSE, MY
days vanish under an avalanche of work. My afternoon
classes—*American Minorities: History, Society, and Politics*
and *Comparative Political Studies*—demand more and more
attention as finals approach.

Whenever some niggling doubt tarnishes the perceived
value of my work, I have one of those glittering days when a
student's tolerance or ethnic pride justifies all my efforts
and I can take the chaff of my life—the lost relationships,
the broken promises, the emotional flotsam of my personal
life—and grind them all underfoot like old cigars. This day,
however, a late Friday in mid-June, is not one of them.

In the morning, Beanie Letterman brought a switchblade to class again. In the afternoon, Ricky Sabine called
me a 'friggin' bitch.' And poor Rosa Ramirez left early for
the third time in as many days. Little Joey was sick again.

On such days, I take to Datha like a moth to a flame.
Their recent *Drift* album eddies in the room now, with all
the escapism of a traveling circus. I've a splodge of Datha

for the eyes too—a short hallway in which I've slung up small autographed posters, snapshots, and the odd personal note from assorted band members.

Ethan has labeled the band my security blanket. Sherika has heartier, more earthy epithets.

It all began so many years ago now, with a fortuitous press conference Datha granted to fanzine editors. This morphed rather magically into a personal relationship with the band that I've treasured for well over a decade now.

In slippers and a frazzled red robe, I zap a stick of French bread pizza in the microwave and pour myself a glass of red wine. Pungent Italian herbs cling to my nostrils like wafts from a cheap pizzeria.

Through the muddle of my apartment, pizza in hand, I pad from the kitchen to the beigey step-down living room, shuffling through an assortment of what I call fan mail, to-gether with hard copies of photos Raine Skype-messaged for possible use on *Conversations'* website.

Emily Richards has e-mailed an emotional piece that reads like prose poetry. Datha empowered her, she says, guiding her toward some personal decision of profound pro-portions. She gives few specifics, but her words are candid, passionate, and uplifting, filled with a soulful gratitude that doesn't drip all over like melted ice cream.

I'm half-embarrassed—as usual—to read what Annie Brenner has sent. Her latest tome is pure fabrication. In a story rife with delusion and questionable detail, she's out-lined—once again—the "very special" encounter she antici-pates having with Raine in Scotland in August, promising details in time.

Chelsea Davis is offering up another poetic plea that gushes and twitches all over with complicated pain, stopped breath, and so forth. Yet from my own experience as a Datha fan, Chelsea's adolescent angst is every bit as valid as

Emily's sharpened self-confidence. It all falls to where we find ourselves in our individual lives at any given time. Chelsea's vulnerable dreams mirror my own at her age. Even now I can say—with all honesty . . . and some chagrin—that I've not yet found a man to equal Raine.

V

FRIDAY NIGHT, EARLY JULY, AND O'CONNELL'S IRISH PUB and Grill crackles with high spirits and loud music. Over the bar hang three stained-glass depictions of leprechauns, and behind, midway between a stack of cut-glass tumblers and a bank of colored cruets and decanters, a central mirror reflects the tri-colored Irish flag. U2 bounces off the moss-green walls as Sherika and I step inside.

"Damn it, he *is* here." A broad-shouldered fellow at the bar, his dark hair tucked under a blue bandana, lifts his glass and grins. "Okay, so he was a bit of a dud, I'll give you that. But then I was no prize either."

Two college-aged lads on either side of the first leer after us as we worm our way across the room.

"Why do I do this to myself?" I shout to Sherika.

"Looking for Mr. Right in all the wrong places," she answers. "Or in your case, Mr. Right Now."

"There . . ." Sherika, on her toes, flags a table at the far end of the room. A darkly handsome man in blue jeans, a tweedy brown jacket, and rust-colored shirt motions back.

"Oh, my God." Even at a distance, I recognize the soft gray eyes, the mild, congenial demeanor. The man's slow smile can still raise a prickle under my skin.

"I know this looks like a gift," Sherika says. "But try to remember, he's here to talk business, not bedrooms."

"Believe me, so am I. He's just familiar, that's all."

"Why am I not surprised? You must have bedded half the city's male population by now."

"Thank you for that fond assessment of my character," I answer with a smirk.

After chats with several other regulars, we arrive at Michael's table. He stands as I drape my jacket across the back of the chair opposite him. His smile deepens as Sherika, settling into the vacant chair between us, makes introductions.

"It's a pleasure," I say, and extend my hand.

"It wasn't. But it could have been," he answers as softly as the bar buzz will allow. He clasps my hand, and the warm smile evaporates as he tightens his grip. "I'm sorry," he says. "I shouldn't have said that. And it *is* a pleasure to meet you." He releases my hand and sits down.

"I seem to have missed something here . . . as usual." Sherika eyes the two of us in turn. "I suppose I should have guessed." She snatches her handbag from the back of her chair and smiles. "Why don't you two settle this? I'm off for drinks."

"Let me, Sherika." Michael jumps up again, digs a wallet out of his tweed jacket, and passes Sherika a thin roll of bills.

"Sit. Talk. Whatever," Sherika says, and vanishes into the crowd.

The man has changed little over the past decade and more. The same smoke-blue eyes. The same firm chin. The hair a tad shorter perhaps. Just brushes his collar now. Not so much California beach boy about him anymore.

"So . . . it's Michael, is it? I don't think we ever got around to first names. Did you know who I was when you met Sherika?"

"Well . . . yes and no. But I know who you were then. Has it really been fifteen years?"

"The hell you did." How presumptuous!

(Fifteen long years past, on the promise of a backstage pass that never materialized, I'd slept with this man's colleague at my very first Datha gig. They were working security.)

"I only mean that right off the bat we should get this Datha thing out of the way, don't you think?" Michael folds his hands on the tabletop. His smug self-confidence is infuriating. "Clear the air, so to speak. Despite what I just said —and I do regret that—it makes no difference to me at all."

I lean in closer to make myself heard. "I propositioned *you* first, as I recall. You turned me down. And that makes no difference?"

"Not to me. We were pretty much kids ourselves. Everyone succumbs to some measure of desperation at least once in a lifetime, especially when they're young. Later, too, for that matter. We all get a little spacey where our dreams are concerned. You should know that better than anyone, from this substance abuse work you've been doing. I hope you've found whatever you thought was missing."

"Is that any of your business?"

"Not a bit. Oops, my song." Before I can protest, Michael has swept me out onto the tiny dance floor, and while Datha's "All That Is" thunders around the room, neither of us has the time or opportunity for conversation. When the song wraps up, I find myself in Michael's arms for a soft, slow U2 number that only magnifies my discomfort.

"Sherika tells me the two of you work together at Irvine." Michael is speaking into my hair, his breath warm and sweet.

"That's right." I search the room for some escape.

"You brought over your own curriculum from Wilmot Junior High, and the school board scooped it up. That's quite a feat."

"It was just a matter of working out something that

would resonate with a high school crowd. Something to spark their curiosity, help them understand themselves . . . each other . . . their choices."

The weather would be next. Too cold for July. Too dry. Another seasonal drought on order. And so on.

"Are we going to chat it up, like what happened all those years ago doesn't matter?"

Michael draws back and studies me. "It doesn't, does it?"

"Most people would say it should."

"I'm not most people. And besides, as I said, you were rattled by a dream. I understood that then. I understand that now. What I've seen since, now *that* I'd call informed realism."

"And what *have* you seen?"

"Well, for starters, about a year ago you spoke at a district school board meeting. You outlined the seeds of this program of yours . . . its rough stages. You were articulate. You were compassionate. You had a sense of humor—something that's always a bonus when you're dealing with serious subjects involving ultra-impulsive, impressionable, hormone-raging teenagers.

"I'd been on the force two or three years by then, and I'd already experienced the countless ways authority fails young people . . . on so many levels. We rarely reach out in any meaningful way. I wasn't even sure what that was until I heard you speak. So when the call came down for volunteers to implement your program, well, I signed up on the spot." Michael releases me briefly and throws up his hands. "And here I am. I'd seen you off and on through the years since the Datha thing, and I knew I'd appreciate a woman who thinks like you do."

"On my back?" I make for our table, but Michael clutches my wrist.

"You know that's not what I meant. Don't be so defensive, Dana. I know what you were doing then. And I know what you're doing now."

"Don't flatter yourself," I say, wrenching my arm free. "And just who the hell do you think you are anyway?"

At the table now, I sling my shoulder bag over the back of my chair and sit down.

"Which one of us hasn't found life more or less contrary to what we expected or hoped for?" Michael says, retaking his own seat.

"Damn it. You don't know me from a brick in the wall. Don't pretend that you do. Ask Sherika. Go ahead . . . ask her."

"Ask Sherika what?" Sherika lowers the cork tray bearing the drinks she's brought from the bar.

"Tell this poor deluded soul what a bitch I can be. And I like it that way. I can take care of myself, thank you very much," I tell Michael. "Always have. Always will. And don't give me any of that vulnerable kitten crap, just to get where you might like to go. I've heard it all before."

"Went for 'whatever,' did we?" Sherika slides a tumbler to either end of the table. "Rum and cokes all around."

"Now who's flattering themselves?" Michael says, and that slow exasperating smile flutters across his lips.

"Why did you come here, anyway?" I ask. "Planning to follow in your friend's footsteps. You are out of your mind. He is out of his mind." I stare at Sherika, who only shrugs and goes back to the bar for nibbles. "Not to mention conceited as hell."

Before I can stop myself, I half stand and toss the contents of my drink in Michael's face.

He sits there stunned for just a moment, and then with great care he unfolds the paper napkin from under his drink and mops his face dry. Worst of all, his smile intensifies.

I spring to my feet and rush around the table, intent on

leaving. But he's already there. He stops in front of me, and my body slams into his. With one fluid motion, he drapes me over his right shoulder, carries me outside, and sets me on my feet by the back door.

"We're all scared sometimes, Dana," he says, bracing a hand to either side of my head. I can feel the warmth of his breath against my cheek. "I'm scared too, sometimes. But that's what life *is* a lot of the time. There's so much more to it—there's so much more to you—than you let anybody see. Accept that. I have."

He smiles again and walks off.

vi

A FEW WEEKS LATER, MID-AUGUST, AND MICHAEL Allyn, who should have dwindled to some half-hearted high-summer amusement, has taken on a disproportionately seductive appeal. He's sussed me out far too well, something which should irk me far more than it does. His charm, his caring, his genuine interest, have all revived my spirits. But more than that, he's just a whole lot of fun. For the first time in years, I actually *want* to make love to someone other than Raine.

That, however, does not seem to be Michael's intent.

We never date. He never stops by. He never calls or texts or e-mails. He never pops up on Facebook or Twitter or Instagram. Whenever we *are* together—either at O'Connell's or at some implementation gathering for the substance abuse program—we always share high, free-wheeling good times. Thoughtful and reflective ones too. I relish this mix. And yet Michael seems to be waiting for something.

"Balderdash." I slam a fist on the kitchen counter, and a

packet of Datha photos flutters to the floor. The autumn digital *Conversations* layout I've been slaving over for hours falls to pieces. I hop off the barstool intent on reconstruction.

Oh, the hell with it. Plenty of time to put the issue to bed. Point . . . click . . . paste. Print and staple for those few hard-copy subscribers. I opt instead for a lengthy, kink-reducing stretch.

And that's when the thin brown envelope propped up beside the microwave collars my attention. I step over and read again, for perhaps the twentieth time:

Dana: Celebrate future with bright and beautiful Hannah McCormick. Upcoming blushing bride. Post-concert reception. September 22nd. MTA, Chicago. Will call when I'm on the coast. Keep a secret. New lives need old friends. Be with me. Love, Raine

When I first opened this note, I'd been wracked with a grievous despair as profound as anything Chelsea Davis might have conjured up from her own misplaced obsession. In retrospect though, my reaction had been rote and rather reflexive: Raine. Pain. Any fifteen-year habit can be hard to break.

On this final run-through, I savor some relief and have come to within a hair's breadth of laying Raine to rest when the front doorbell chimes. Michael Allyn, in an earth-brown trench coat and a rust-colored shirt and tie, lounges in the doorway, one arm propped high against the doorjamb.

My heart flinches . . . but I'll never let him know.

"Are you lost?" I ask.

"Just in the neighborhood," he says. "Thought I might take you to dinner tonight, say eight o'clock? If you're of a mind and not already spoken for."

This first from Michael blindsides me, but I finger Raine's invitation, still in hand.

I've lost him. Then again, I never really had him. Do I deserve a second chance . . . a third . . . a fourth . . . with any decent man? Can I risk it? Do I want to?

"I'll be bad company," I say.

"So . . . I'll be good."

"How good?" I lean into Michael, my fingers fiddling with the front buttons of his shirt. "And at what?" I can still play the game.

"We'll just have to wait and see now, won't we?" Michael's head dips to mine, and his lips brush my temple. "Take your track shoes off, Dana," he whispers.

"What?" I give him a playful shove, but he only smiles and lazes against the doorjamb again, his arms folded on his chest.

"You break them out whenever anybody gets too close. You do this vamp thing, this bad girl thing that helps you stay in control. You're getting ready to run, aren't you?"

"Shelve the shrink act, Michael." I swipe at his crossed arms with the back of my hand. "I'm a bad risk. You know it. I know it. I'll mess up your life. Your career, too, if I can manage it. I'm just no good with men." I reach up and brush his cheek. "But we shouldn't let my reputation go to waste, should we?"

Michael's smile evaporates. "Stop it, Dana," he murmurs.

My heart leaps into my throat, and I ache to take him in my arms.

"Gotta run," he says suddenly. "Be back at eight."

And he's gone.

vii

—

JUST AFTER NINE O'CLOCK, WE EAT A LATE DINNER AT THE San Diego Seafood Emporium in Seaport Village, down on the docks. We sit at an upstairs table of polished honey-gold pine, the windows open to a salty sea breeze. Hurricane lamps soften the room, and the bay breathes rhythmically under the full moon.

As a rule, I avoid Seaport Village. Too much unmanageable romance. Too many overstimulating sea breezes, babbling brooks, and so forth. Tonight, a riot of late summer flowers and mellowed lamplight suffuse the place with a fairy-tale expectancy, and calf-eyed couples drift down cobblestoned walkways, meandering past balloon stalls and soda fountains, carousels and book niches. All of this threatens my objectivity.

"I'd have to agree." I step back into the night from the Seaport Bookstop and Café, *Poems from the Scottish Hills* tucked under my arm. "Like everyone else, kids hunger for some sense of control in their lives, however tenuous. That's one of the many things that appealed to me about tweaking the criminal justice system to deal with juvenile substance abuse."

Hand in hand, Michael and I round a corner of the boardwalk and come face-to-face with the sea. The blackened bay glitters like shattered glass, and we linger in the shadow of a smoke tree.

"My God." I place a hand on Michael's chest. "Look at the moonlight on the water. I can't tell you how long it's been since I even cared about a full moon."

I close my eyes, draw in a breath of tangy sea air, and when Michael kisses me, it comes as no surprise.

Instead, I feel relief . . . a deep, deep gratitude. And something very close to happiness. All my life I've yearned for this kiss. A blissful honeyed contentment washes over me.

Layered on the rush of this kiss, however, comes a thin string of bleeps that dribbles down my backbone like ice crystals.

"Damn," Michael says into my open mouth.

"Was that your phone?"

Michael releases me and pulls a cell phone from the inside pocket of his trench coat. One tap and the chirping stops.

On tiptoe, I kiss the corner of his mouth. "Why the hell here. And why now?"

That familiar slow smile lights Michael's eyes. "I am a homicide detective, remember?"

"And you're on duty?"

"Afraid so. I suppose I should have mentioned that. Sorry."

Michael checks in with his precinct, and we circle back to the Camaro. "An incident just down on the dock here," he explains. "We're in such close range, so to speak. Shouldn't take long."

South of Seaport Village, a line of enormous steel-walled dockland warehouses presses its back to the sea. As we approach, a maze of flashing colored lights defines the darkness. Three police cruisers in a semicircle direct their headlights into the delivery entrance of RAMCO, INC., the name rusting over the doorway in thick black letters. Four officers mill about what looks like a man's body blanketed on the pavement.

Fumbling for a cigarette, I put a hand to my mouth.

"Wait here." Michael pulls a notepad from his trench coat as he steps out of the car.

I crank open my window. "What have you got?" is all I catch before an offshore breeze blows his words away.

The body on the ground lies motionless. Blood, black and oily in the headlights of the cruisers, stains the pavement.

One of the officers motions further up the docks, into the warehouse, and then toward a tiny glass-enclosed security station just inside the entrance. A fifth officer crouches in the doorway there, rising as Michael approaches, and I spot a dark-haired girl hunkered in the corner, a toddler on one knee, a pistol in her right hand. Without looking away, I fumble for the Camaro's ashtray and snuff out my cigarette. Squinting over the dashboard, I strain to make out the young woman's face, but she dissolves in a murky blur. Two of the officers shift position then, blocking my view altogether.

Despite my better judgment—and Michael's orders—I crack open the car door, slip outside, and creep along the far side of the Camaro, groping my way to the rear of the nearest cruiser, my eyes locked on the gathering ahead.

"She won't talk," the officer nearest the cubicle says. "And she won't give up the piece."

Michael nods toward the body on the ground, and my eyes follow. "Carlos here is her old man. Came to pick the bastard up. He shuts down for the night watchman? I'm guessing the deal goes south. Carlos gets plugged. The girl goes bonkers. Snags the stuff. Snags the piece and hides."

"That's the long and short of it," one of the officers says. "Just a kid. Fifteen, maybe sixteen. Scared shitless."

Michael edges closer to the cubicle and crouches down.

My eyes fixed on the dark hair obscuring the girl's face, I hold my breath and steal along the left side of the cruiser.

One more step and I'd have had a clear view, when to my everlasting horror, my foot snags a discarded aluminum can that shoots up into the air, bounces off the left front tire of the first cruiser, and dribbles out into the headlights.

The girl jumps. With the snap of firecrackers, two bullets slam into the ceiling of the cubicle.

Everyone has dropped to the ground, spread-eagled, their guns divided between me—frozen in the circle of cruiser headlights—and the young girl, her hand wrapped around her smoking gun. The baby on her lap reaches out toward the muzzle.

I gulp down a mouthful of air.

At the end of an infinite silence, the girl stands up. "Miss Morrison?" she says.

I edge closer.

Anger and shock distort Michael's face, but he, too, slowly comes to his feet.

The girl in the cubicle remains motionless, and one by one, the officers stand, their legs splayed, their guns drawn with their arms extended.

The girl's dark eyes widen with fear, and she draws the baby closer, the gun still in her right hand, at arm's length.

I slump against the cruiser's front door and wait.

Michael signals to the other officers, and they each put up their weapon. "Do you know this woman?" he says, motioning me forward.

My breath rapid and shallow, I step up. The girl in the cubicle tosses back her hair, and I recognize her at once.

"Rosa? Rosa Ramirez," I tell the others without looking back. "She's one of my students."

I slip past Michael as Rosa pushes herself to her feet. The baby, still balanced on her left hip, nibbles on his mother's arm. I lean in the doorway and brush his plump cheek. "So, this is Joey?" The baby pulls my finger toward his open mouth. "Carlos will be okay, Rosa." I glance over my shoulder, and Michael nods. "Do you know what he was doing here?"

The girl shakes her head, her eyes sliding to the knot of men behind me.

"It's okay. You can tell us."

"He was going to be late," Rosa says. "That's all I know. I was supposed to pick him up . . . after eleven. But I came early, and this man was here with Carlos. He said I was with the cops. And then he shot Carlos and split." The gun droops. Rosa shivers, sniffs, and wipes her reddened eyes.

Outside, one of the officers shifts, and the gun bounces up again.

"It's alright, Rosa." I stroke Joey's arm.

"I don't know anything, Miss Morrison. I swear." Rosa's eyes tear up and her lips quiver. "Carlos does these things. He won't tell me. I think I'll get away sometimes, but it's just too hard."

"I know. Did you see the man who shot Carlos?" Rosa nods. I rub the baby's back, and he lets out a string of soft coos. "These men can help you, I promise. Please give it up, Rosa. For Joey. For yourself."

Rosa's eyes drift over the baby's face. Seconds stretch into an eternity, but in the end, she hands the gun to me, and I pass it back to Michael. And then Rosa and little Joey fall together into my arms.

An ambulance has arrived, and, after a flurry of activity, some animated and intense discussion among officers and paramedics—all under Michael's supervision—the "incident" is brought to a close. "Have someone from Victim Witness over there to meet them," Michael orders. "And I want a full report on my desk in the morning."

Another night watchman is called in to take up Carlos's post, and one by one the squad cars fade into the night. Two slip away in opposite directions, and the third, with Rosa and Joey, trails the ambulance.

"Certainly does get the adrenaline pumping," I say to Michael as we head back to the car. "I *am* sorry, Michael."

We pull away from the dock, but he's so quiet that I'm

wracked with fear. "I'll never do anything that stupid again. I promise."

(He'll be gone now, like all the others. And, damn it, this is one man I don't want to go.)

"I know what you're thinking. It was irresponsible and dangerous and stupid. Someone could have been killed. I know that."

"*You* could have been killed," Michael says. "Joey could have been killed. Rosa. One of my officers."

"I know."

"I know you better than you know yourself," he says. "And it *won't* ever happen again."

Tears flood into my eyes. Dana Morrison strikes out . . . again. Outside my window, city lights blur into a wash of silver and gold. Why am I always so headstrong, when for once in my life someone matters so much?

"It won't happen again." Michael's jaw slackens, his grip on the wheel loosens a hair, and I dare to hope. "It won't happen again because you're too smart for that." When he turns to me, he almost smiles. "And no, you don't know what I'm thinking."

He pulls the Camaro north onto the oceanside freeway. "A piece of luck, I'll grant you that . . . in so many, many ways. And I don't condone an ounce of it. You know that. But once in there, you were good." His eyes soften. "I was impressed. What a great outlet for all of that anger and excess energy. We could use you on the team, so to speak."

My breath seeps out in silent pulses, and I wet my lips. "What anger? I'm not angry at all. In fact, I'm feeling something else altogether."

"I don't mean now. I mean angry in general."

The flash of city lights whips along the roadside, golden against the brushy hills. "I suppose you're right," I admit, and a weight like chain mail lifts off my shoulders. "A lot of people don't give me credit for real feelings. So I give them what they expect. That makes me angry sometimes, I guess."

"Admit it now," Michael says. "You do your damnedest to hold yourself back, afraid you'll get hurt. I'd say that makes you pretty normal. But look at what can happen when you let go. Now that's the woman who caught my attention at that first school board meeting."

I smile through another silence while moonlight silvers the low hills.

"You should follow your own advice," Michael says.

"Hmm?"

"Take the consequences of your own actions. If you don't like the consequences, change the actions."

"Damn it, don't go all wobbly on me now, Michael. I'm feeling too good. And where the hell are we going?"

"A nice quiet little place I know."

"If you're thinking of a frolic in a four-poster, you're taking a hell of a lot for granted."

"Now who's jumping to conclusions?" Michael grins. "A four-poster is out of the question. For the moment anyway. Almost there."

We sweep down out of the coastal woods. Below and to the left, the long narrow strand of Torrey Pines Beach glows in the moonlight. Erratic lines of breakers, shredded into glassy shards, etch the black water with a shatter of glistening white foam. Michael parks off the road at the bottom of the hill. The roadside, the beach, the sea, all lie empty and immense before us.

Hand in hand, we set off across the pale sand. When we reach the flatness where high tide has been, I flick off my shoes. Michael does too.

The water swirls in wide bubble-edged arches that tinge my feet with coolness. The hiss. The rush. The thunderous pounding. The boiled fizz of retreat. As the seas come and go, we pull each other through the waves in turn.

"So, what are these feelings that people don't give you credit for?" Michael asks over the roar of the breakers.

The ocean has begun to soothe me, a luxury I haven't allowed myself in years. *Standing silver in the wind, like blown glass.*

"Being real, I guess." The rhythm of the waves echoes and re-echoes around us. "It's beautiful here, isn't it?" I stand alone at the edge of the surf. "Like a dream, only better, because it's all real. Oh, I don't know." I start off again. "The feelings everybody has, I guess. Being hurt. Being afraid. Being lonely."

"It only matters what *you* think, you know." Michael's hand tightens on mine, and he pulls me off down the beach, water curling around our ankles. "You do hurt," he says.

"I do."

"And you're afraid sometimes."

"I am."

"And lonely."

"Yes!" I shout over the waves.

"Let it out, Dana. You can, you know."

"I *am* like everyone else."

"You are."

"I need the same things."

"You do."

"I want the same things."

"Yes."

"I hope and I care and I hurt and I love."

"Here's the third wave, Dana!" Michael shouts. "The biggest and the best. Let's go." He sweeps me into his arms and whirls me over the water. We spin like madmen in the moonlight. "Let it out," he says.

We scream together then, out there over the bright water. A primal explosion of sound. A catharsis of anger, frustration, fear, hope, joy.

The release for me is complete, and when we make love in the grass above the beach, I'm reborn. Everything I've known has become far too sharp to ever have been real.

But I'm up for air now. And it feels more than right.

Chelsea's Story

(In Her Own Words)

i

FOR APRIL'S GOLD RUSH MEETING, WE'VE GATHERED IN the rec room of my UT dorm for a showing of the Datha bootleg *Drift and Misery*. We've only been around a few years, Gold Rush, but we've got some five hundred and fifty dues-paying members. Most of them are computer geeks who never make a monthly get-together, but we're still Toronto's top Datha fan club, and I'm chuffed about that.

Two other club contenders hang in the mix: Wishes for Tomorrow (WTF, I call them), which took its name from a track on Datha's third album, *Walls for the Wind,* and raises money for human rights groups (too single-minded for me); and Delirium, named for a song from Datha's second album, *The Fire.* They promote local bands with benefit concerts for area charities. Not heavy enough on Datha's own music for me. Even five years ago, half a dozen fanzines claimed the city. Social media squelched most of those.

Gold Rush sprang from the Boston Datha group, Halftones, a name they snatched from Datha's fourth album, *Three Candles.* Halftones has an online fanzine, but its emphasis is local, with regular food drives, Christmas toys, baby food, that sort of thing. Their platform is built around Datha's own lyrics.

Gold Rush does all of that and more, and I feel hugely connected to the group. It's easy to step out of myself here— but not far enough to fall. Sure, members throw some shade on each other now and then about causes and priorities, but on the whole, I think we rock. I mean, we're pretty lit.

Tonight, we're deep into a blistering rendition of "Speaking Eyes" from Datha's current Drift Tour. Massey Hall, April 25. Raine's roaring into the darkness: "*Were you the light when I touched the sky? Speaking eyes?*"

"Speaking eyes," the on-screen crowd echoes, and we rave right back. The video's from a smartphone way up in the nosebleed section on the far left, so there's jostling and jumping, and, where "Speaking Eyes" always gives me the feels, I've already got a massive headache.

Raine drags a hand through his hair. It's glistening with sweat. And then he blares out something none of us can make out.

But, wow, can I dance! I mean, I really cut loose, totally cray. But then I catch just a snip of that new guy, Nicki. He's totally chill, but I can't look at him or he'll swallow me whole. I know I'm blushing, so I punch back my glasses and howl so loud my throat hurts.

The camera goes a bit nutty at this point, skimming over the tops of heads, and then lodges on Dirk, pounding away at his drum kit. Left of center, Graeme throws out some kick-ass guitar riffs, and then there's a big lurch over to Colin, on bass. He's prowling like a caged lion at the far right of the stage. I could die right here, drowning in that sound.

"*Are you the candle I read you by? Speaking eyes!*"

"Speaking eyes!"

I'm blown away when Nicki grabs my arm, and then we're on the floor together.

He's thin faced and boyish, and his wispy dirt-blond hair just touches the top of his shoulders. "Speaking Eyes" is his favorite *Drift* single, he shouts to me. I beam back and nod that it's mine too.

"Are you a part of the truth I seek? Are you a mark on the wisdom tree? Speaking eyes."

Nicki's eyes sweep down along my cheekbone and across my lips, and I know I'm flushed all over again.

Focus. Focus. Focus. Stay with the words.

A wisdom tree. What's that? A tree of knowledge?

Now there's a killer idea. Why not whip up some Gold Rush energy for Toronto's literacy campaign? Could be a fab Gold Rush project.

ii
##

TORONTO'S IN THE GRIP OF AN OUT-OF-SEASON LATE May heat wave. The air's waterlogged and oppressive, and I'm dripping with sweat. The smallest move is an effort. I struggle to even breathe.

Despite the limp heat, Datha, on-screen for Gold Rush's May meeting (the LA Forum, June 17, the Walls for the Wind Tour), can still bring me to my feet. Solo dancing is really my thing. I can suck the music right into my brain and my body and let the words take over. No distractions. Nobody's thirsty attitude—not even Nicki's.

Especially not Nicki's. It's frightening and confusing to me that I'm so into him.

On the other hand, I'm pretty sure it's love.

"All That Is" comes up on-screen. *"Wetness in a northern world,"* Raine rasps. Whistles and hoots flood in from the audience. But there, where he stands alone, center stage, in a single bluish glow like moonlight, there's only his voice. His white shirt, full and blousy, is unlaced at the neckline,

open at the cuffs, gleaming as pure and immaculate as freshly fallen snow. The black leather pants, the inky sleekness of
his hair, meld into a shock of darkness. He splays his legs.
He lowers his head. He grips the microphone stand.

"*On the road from Brachloch,*"—it's like an invocation
—"*when all the over-watching hills were young, you passed
homeward in the night, all knowing.*" He looks to the left. He
looks to the right. The crowds go nuts.

"*From the final flash of day, you stood silver in the wind,
like blown glass.*" It's like a prayer, really. Like he's been
zapped by some spiritual power.

A blast of brilliant white, and the stage convulses with
pyrotechnics. Fragments of light expand upward and out.
Cell phones blink through the darkness like a zillion fireflies.
Lasers spin around the room, bounce off the ceiling, shower
the pulsing crowd, and then swivel up again.

Totally savage!

Raine's doubled over now, one hand on his microphone
stand. He flings it sideways, backwards, to the floor. Dirk's
drums rattle the walls, Graeme's guitar wails like a banshee,
and Colin's bass pounds out a string of primitive throbs.

Two and a half hours later, when the concert ends, the
whole room is spent. Energy glows on each face like radia-
tion.

"Great stuff!" To whistles and hoots, Stephanie Higgins
steps to the front of the room. "Nice going, Chel," she says.

"It was Dana Morrison, really." At the back of the room,
I push up my glasses once again. "She couldn't use the last
poem I messaged over. I guess she felt bad about that. She
had this totally sick bootleg from LA. Nothing online yet. I
knew we had to have one."

"And what about all those tight shots of Raine?" Stephi
adds.

"Great stuff, alright." Samantha Higgins fires up the overhead lights, and the room drops to a rumble. "But we don't have all night here, eh? We should get down to business."

They're identical twins, Stephi and Sam. Sam shaves her chestnut hair nearly to the bone, where Stephi lightens hers —shoulder-length and flouncy—to the color of ripened wheat. The Bald and the Beautiful, I call them. Stephi loves that. Sam . . . not so much.

Sam's outfits are snatch—black, black, black, even in this heat wave. Black pants, black Datha T-shirt and vest, black felt bolero, black suede ankle boots, and a row of black beads outlining her left ear.

So much black in one place conjures up a funereal vibe, Stephi says. Mars the reputation Datha has for introspection, inspiration, cautious optimism, and all of that. Stephi's always on fleek. Totally Gucci. Her favorite color is a blazing scarlet, which she wears in silk blouses and swirling peasant skirts. Stephi's earrings can range from miniature wind chimes to parrot feathers.

In my oversized men's dress shirts and blue jeans, I'm more of an afterthought next to the twins. I fancy myself with more of a floppy hipness anyway. I guess the only thing we really have in common is that we're all vegetarians.

When someone bawls, "Get a grip, Sam," from the back of the room, the muttering doubles up.

"For God's sake, Sam," Stephi gripes, rolling her eyes. "Lighten up, will ya. Give us a chance to digest this stuff. You know what Datha concerts are like."

"I think Sam's right," I say. "We have a lot to get done." Only Nicki is listening. He smiles back, and my heart is pounding for the lost puppy look in his eyes.

"Don't get your knickers in a twist," Stephi tells her sister, and heads off for the kitchen, crooking her finger for me and Nicki to follow.

From a corner cupboard, she takes down a dozen small

pretzel bags and the half-emptied cookie tin from April's meeting. "Do these up for me, will you, Chel? You know where the pop is. Probably flat. Paper cups where they always are. Just throw it all together like you usually do. PDQ, eh?"

When she leaves, I dump shortbread, ginger cookies, and fig bars onto a long plastic platter. Nicki helps, and the brush of his hand on mine raises a prickle of heat across my scalp.

"I'll put out the drinks." Nicki tucks his limp hair behind his ears and hauls up an assortment of half-empty pop bottles from under the sink. "We work good together, don't we, Chel? We could be the refreshment committee."

"We *are* the refreshment committee." I try to laugh, but he's leaning in front of me now, his face just inches away.

"I hope we settle this Eaton thing tonight," Nicki says. "It's a great idea." He opens a bag of crushed ice and sets it in the sink. "You come up with such popping stuff, Chel. What would we do without you?"

"Ah, you'd all do just fine."

"No, really," Nicki says. "You inspire a lot of people, Chel. With your enthusiasm. People know where you stand, how much things mean to you." He whips off his hat—a Toronto Blue Jays baseball cap worn backwards—worms his skinny fingers through his hair, and plops the cap back on. "Whatta you say we take in a movie Friday night?"

My heart trips all over itself, and I work to contain a smile that's spilling into my eyes. "I don't know," I say. "Don't you have to work?"

"Friday's a Burger 'n' Bun day. Just a side hustle. I can switch with Charlie on a dime. I hate that Friday night shift anyway. They got this two-burger special, so we get gobs of customers. Way too much work for me." He laughs, and then his slight body sags. "But you probably got some handsome hunk hanging around the house all the time these days, eh?"

"No," I say—much too quickly. "I don't . . . really." Derek Lamont has been the closest thing to a hunk I've ever come to. He asked me to the senior prom last year when Stephi got the measles. Ended up chasing Caprice Williams all night after I spilled spiked punch down the front of my dress.

"We could go over a song list," Nicki says.

"I'll have to let you know. Is that alright?"

"Sure. Text me."

"God's truth now," Sam is saying when we head back to the other room. "We gotta get serious here, or the whole night'll be gone." She pops out the LA DVD and snaps it back in its jewel case. "Last month somebody—was it you, Chel? Somebody brought up expanding the online newsletter, instead of these mass e-mails. We'd just have to send out a notification with a link. Maybe we need to get more active with the Facebook page, too, and concentrate more on putting the band's words and ideas into practice."

I raise a hand, but Stephi brushes me off.

"What's the big hairy deal, Sam?" she says. "There's a lot of levels to Datha's music. What's wrong with the 'God, they're gorgeous' one? Add a few sexy photos. Maybe a bit of humor. We're so goddamn serious all the time."

Voices break out everywhere, and Stephi shushes the room. "Chelsea's got something to say. Go ahead, Chel," she says.

"Just a thought. I know we get together and we do have a bit of fun. But isn't it more about being inspired by the music?"

"Totally," Sam says. "More people need to hear what these guys have to say, eh?" She throws out a call then for each member present to text in some inspirational Datha quote for the next newsletter.

"I've been looking into this literacy thing," Stephi says. "And I think we ought to go ahead with it."

Nicki drops down beside me on the couch, and I have to shift away to stay on point. "We've been helping out with one-on-one tutoring for a couple of months now," Stephi continues. "And I think that's fab. We need to keep that up. But I was talking to Earl yesterday. He says that Literacy Advocates can't keep the building open much longer. You know—lights, electricity, water. Stuff like that. Busking could really help them out."

The room mumbles its approval.

"So . . . every weekend next month, what say me, Chelsea, Sam, and Nicki head over to Eaton Centre . . . some place downtown. We do this right into September. Right up until Datha's concert at Midwest Telecom in Chicago on the twenty-second. We might even make enough to pay their utility bills."

"Way to go, Steph!" someone calls from the back of the room. "You're always dope."

We all agree then, that given permission from mall management, Nicki, Stephi, Sam, and me—in the name of Gold Rush—will busk for small change at Eaton Centre. We'll rehearse Thursday and Friday nights, until the school year wraps up, and then hit the streets off and on through summer school, until the fall semester fires up.

That decided, Gold Rush adjourns.

iii
—

MY MOTHER, MYRNA DAVIS, DRAGS A BIG-TOOTHED COMB through my hair, separating out a swatch from which she snips off a half inch or more. And then she measures out a second section of equal width.

"I'm sure he's a lovely boy, dear," she says. "But your

father and I have to be at the club early this evening. We *will* meet him sometime though. Don't you worry."

She pats my shoulder, measures again, snips again. "Why don't you wear that navy-blue pants outfit Grandma Davis gave you for Christmas last year? Your father's never liked that color on you, I know. But then, like so much of the male corporate world, fashion's never been his forte, has it? It's a lovely outfit. Doesn't make you look so thin. Better that than these old rags from Goodwill." She fingers my overlarge dress shirt as if it were someone else's dirty laundry. "Yes, go with the blue," she says. "You can always take along a jacket. I must say, this has been the coolest July in years. Is this the same young man you've been seeing the past month or so? Works at the Sub Factory? His parents are in town?"

"No . . . he's on his own. Never talks about his family, like I said before. There's something about him that makes me so sad."

"I'm just glad to see you getting out more, dear." My mother leans back, assessing, with her sharp hazel eyes, the sleek hair now framing my face.

"He's a bit lonely, I think . . . He dances just with me every meeting. Did I tell you?"

"There now, dear. You look very smart. Yes . . . let's go with the navy blue. Doesn't make you look so emaciated."

iv
—

WE'RE TO MEET STEPHI AND SAM AT THE EATON CENTRE'S north-side entrance at six thirty, so with half an hour to spare, Nicki and I stop for coffee at a quirky little diner on Yonge Street. Nicki's hands flutter a lot, and his smile seems strained. But he's as vulnerable as ever to me, and I'm so excited to be sharing time and friendship with him. Feeling useful. Significant.

I'm alert to his every mood and mind-shift—we are, after all, *dating*—so this tweak in temperament puzzles me at first. But I write it off to stage fright.

A bone-cold early September rain threatens. Low marbled clouds clamp down on the city like damp cotton. No rain comes, however, and though the sky remains wintry-looking, we're determined to go ahead with our Saturday night session.

The Centre, multi-tiered in metal and glass, boils with shoppers and browsers. All ages. All energies. All dispositions.

"This is so much better than last weekend with all that Blue Jays competition," Stephi says. "A killer vibe for attracting some good-cause small change, eh?"

"Those neon duds of yours can't hurt either," Sam tells her sister with a bit of a leer. Stephi's crimson velvet beret and scarlet shawl, together with Nicki's oversized red Datha T-shirt and Sam's eye-popping bald pate, are sure to attract attention, as always.

When the Centre closes, we take our act over to West Queen, where I'm blown away as usual by the wild atmosphere. Stephi, Sam, and Nicki take it all in stride, unfazed and unimpressed.

"You gotta get out more, Chel." Stephi slings my embroidered guitar strap over my head. "These people deal and pimp and God knows what else down here late at night." She ducks back to the front window of the music shop we've chosen as our next venue. "Oh, lord," she mumbles. "It's Ishua."

"Who?" I fling a few coins into my open guitar case, centered midway between Nicki and myself.

"That old man's been a fixture down here for years," Stephi says.

In a deep maroon robe, Ishua, with long hair, wild blue

eyes, and a frazzled beard like Moses on Mt. Sinai, charges at us, a staff in one hand, a Bible in the other.

"*The whole world lieth in wickedness.*" He's pushed his face so close to mine that I can see the gold fillings in his teeth.

"What?" I say.

"*There is none righteous, not one.*"

"Pay no attention, Chel. He talks like that all the time." Stephi tugs at the old man's beard. "He's got the whole world on his shoulders, don't you, Ishua?"

The old guy fixes his blinding gaze on Stephi, and his brow crinkles. "*That women adorn themselves in modest apparel. Not with gold or pearls or costly array, but with good works. Beauty is vain.*" He stabs his staff on the pavement, nearly impaling my right foot, and I step back into Nicki's arms, my guitar resting against his thigh.

"No gold here, old man." Stephi laughs. "Costly array? Well . . . maybe. These duds ain't cheap, dude."

"Ah, let the old fart alone," Sam says. "We got work to do."

I've just begun to relax in Nicki's arms when he steps out from behind me. "What makes you think you've cornered the market on good deeds, old man?" he asks, his body shriveling beside the old man now glowering down on him.

"Works of the devil. Devil's work . . . with these vile instruments." Ishua flaps his opened Bible toward my guitar. "*Ye that chant to the sound of the viol and invent to themselves instruments of music, now shall they go captive.*"

"Hold on, sport," Nicki says. "*Make a joyful noise unto the Lord,* isn't that what your good book says?"

"*He that loveth pleasure shall be a poor man.*"

"Well . . . *blessed are the poor,*" Nicki snaps back. I look across to Stephi and Sam. Are they as proud of Nicki's spunk as I am?

Ishua falters. "Whose songs do you sing here anyway?"

he asks. "*The works of the flesh are manifest, which are these —drunkenness and reveling. Their works are in darkness.*"

"You don't know jack shit about the songs we sing," Nicki says.

"*The corrupt tree bringeth forth evil fruit. Whoever will be a friend of the world is the enemy of God.*"
"Then *love your enemies*," Nicki spits back.

For a long moment, Ishua blinks with confusion. "*Men loved darkness rather than the light . . . because their deeds were evil.*"

"So what the hell are you doing out here, you fucking pervert?" Nicki shouts, as Ishua turns to leave. "Looks pretty damn dark out here to me."

Crooked over his staff, Ishua shuffles off down the street, shaking his head.

"Good job, Nicki." Stephi claps Nicki's shoulder, but he jerks his arm away.

"Who the hell does he think he is anyway? He's no better than the rest of us, the fucking bastard."

Stephi passes Sam a long, hard glare. "Let's pack it in for the night then, eh?" she says.

But Nicki just stands there, staring after Ishua.

V

"THREE HUNDRED CLAMS PLUS," STEPHI SAYS. "NOT BAD for our last night's work, eh? We're down to the wire with fall semester starting up next week."

"Hey!" I jab Sam's shoulder. "Maybe after the concert in Chicago, we could get back into it, keep it up till Christmas. I mean, really go at it for the holidays."

"Great idea, Chel," Sam says. "Bring that up next month."

I drop down to one knee and snap my guitar case shut. "It's been a lot of fun, hasn't it?" I say to Nicki.

He tucks his harmonica into a pocket of his denim jacket as I get to my feet. "Totally lit. Best set ever." He blows his breath onto a shop-front window and scrawls *DATHA* in the steamy droplets. "Whatta you say to some coffee, Chel?"

Stephi and Sam trade beamy smirks, and I blush.

"Great," I say. "You guys wanna come?"

"Nah . . . It's after eleven. We'll catch you later," Stephi says. "Let's have the guitar, Chel. You'll wanna have your hands free." She winks, takes the case, and nudges her sister toward the nearest subway station, and after long and fervent goodbyes, she and Sam are gone.

I wander back along West Queen with Nicki, and we settle into a glitzy all-night diner, empty but for one other couple. Sitting in a booth by the window, we gaze in silence at the cold, damp, early September night. I'm glowing with the good things done.

As lost-looking as ever, Nicki's innocence touches me all over again, and I feel protective and important.

We order. I prop my chin in the palm of one hand and scan the lamplit street. "Look at that poor old thing over there by the bus stop." I tap the windowpane with a knuckle, and my spirits fizzle.

Across the street, an elderly woman in a tattered overcoat and oversized rubber boots is poking around in a garbage bin with a long metal bar something like a tire iron.

"The suffering in this city always amazes me," I say. "Totally needless. Don't you just feel overwhelmed sometimes? Like nothing you do can ever make a difference?"

"A lot of things *you* do make a big difference to me, Chel."

"Really? Honest?" I sit back as the waitress hands off two black coffees.

"I'm serious."

I rap my fingers on the tabletop until the old woman outside disappears down an alley. "I don't do anything really," I say. "And sometimes I'm so confused myself. What should Gold Rush do? Where should we put our efforts and our time and our energy? What's best to do for myself? Datha sorta guides me that way. They show me the way. Is that weird or what?"

"No. I think that's great." Nicki whips off his Blue Jays cap, runs a hand through his hair, and slaps the cap back on. "I mean you've made a big difference to me." He leans forward and studies my face, and for a second I think he's going to cry. "I've never told anyone this before." He glances to either end of the room. "When I was a kid, my mom never gave me the slightest bit of attention. I mean ever. She drank a lot. I never really knew who she was. One day, right after my fourteenth birthday, she just disappeared."

Tears flood into my eyes.

"I mean, I came in from school one day and . . . well . . . she just never came home. I've been on my own ever since." Nicki covers my hand with his, and my heart rockets right up into my throat. "You've thrown yourself into Gold Rush, and you still get so much out of it. Maybe . . ." Nicki's voice fades away.

"Maybe you can too? Of course, you can. It's all of us together. Each of us. We can all make a difference. Small change really *can* add up, you know." I'm self-conscious now, and I pull my hand back. "We're all part of the same truth. We're all a mark on the wisdom tree."

Nicki's body slumps. "I sort of see it. But where do I start?"

I'm bubbling over with Datha idealism now. "Just be the best person you can be. Nobody else can do that. Look at what we did this summer. Totally popping, eh? And . . . we couldn't have done that without *you*."

"It all sounds too simple."

Panic grips my chest. The right words are there, if only I can remember them.

"Sometimes the band talks to me," I say. "I mean just to me. Like they created something just for me. The music inspires me in a very specific way. Do you know what I mean? I listen. And things just come. Pretty weird, eh?"

I glance out the window again.

"Like this whole literacy thing?" (Yes, the literacy thing. Thank God something bubbled up.)

"That whole idea came to me right after Datha's Chicago concert back in April. We played a Massey Hall video at our meeting that month. Remember? And that got me thinking about the wisdom tree in "Speaking Eyes"? You know—a tree of knowledge, like in the Bible. So . . . literacy. How could Gold Rush help out in some way? There's just so much there if you really listen."

"I can try, I guess."

We finish our coffee in silence.

"How about now?" Nicki says at last. He shoots forward and snatches my arm. "Come over to my place, Chel. I've got this killer stereo. We could listen to the old stuff and you could show me how it all happens, this inspiration. Whatta you say, Chel?"

A complicated surge of power rushes to my head.

"I guess. But I have to be home before two or Stephi and Sam get all paranoid. You know we *should* listen to the old stuff. There's so much more there."

"Whatever," Nicki says. And so it's decided.

We reach Nicki's building off Blair Boulevard in under twenty minutes. There's a Dickensian vibe about the place. Four stories of grim blasted brick dulled by soot. No windows. The entrance, off a garbage-strewn blind alley, oozes steam like malarial mist, and the atmosphere is dystopian. I'm exhilarated, feeling even a bit risqué.

The door creaks open with just a touch, and I peer into a hallway pocked with skid marks and grease, like lichen on a rock. Chicken wire cradles an inside light fixture hanging from the ceiling. Broken walls expose lumps of crumbling plaster, rotted wood beams, and a snake's nest of colored wires. The smell falls somewhere between my grandparents' root cellar and the latrines in UT's football stadium.

I shiver but step inside.

We make our way down a chipped cement staircase at the far end of the hallway and enter the basement, where Nicki pushes open a plank door.

"It's not much," he says. "But it's all I can afford—which is nothing. I've been squatting here for a couple of months now. Looks like I'll be gone soon though. Yesterday, somebody tacked up a condemnation notice. Don't know where I'll end up then? Hash slingers and bottle washers don't rake in much cash." His voice has slipped into bitterness. "Minimum wage and greasy burgers. No posh college cafeteria for me."

I squirm with guilt.

My parents' Edwardian home on Indian Grove near High Park has given me a comfortable, predictable life. My mother, an English prof at the U, orders all of our groceries by phone. My father—Harold Willard Joseph Davis III, a lifelong corporate man—has his three-piece suits tailored by a gay couple who stop by at regular intervals of twelve to eighteen months. Punctual as the phases of the moon.

And from some exotic quarter of the city, a shy East Indian scrubwoman named Indira materializes once a week to return the house to pristine perfection. Only once do I ever remember it being otherwise. On my sixteenth birthday, Margot Anderson dumped a piece of chocolate mousse on Pauly Bender's head. Some of that mouse soiled the champagne carpet for over an hour.

Nicki's place is not like that. A cubicle in the bottom

left-hand corner of the building, it measures about ten square feet. A stained mattress hugs the floor opposite the door, and beside this, there's a stereo with speakers in each corner of the room. Midway down the right wall, stacks of red plastic milk crates have been crammed with crumpled clothes. In front of these sits a puce-colored armchair, oozing stuffing from rifts in the seat cushion. The dripping of water filters out from behind a set of gauzy blue curtains left of the door. Styrofoam and paper cups, cigarette butts, crumpled newspapers, and cardboard pizza containers litter the rug remnant on the floor.

"Sorry about the mess." Nicki gathers up a half dozen flattened cardboard boxes and stuffs them behind the mattress. Tossing off his jacket, he sits back on his heels and swivels toward me. "How about *Walls for the Wind*? I've always liked "Wishes for Tomorrow" from that album. And of course, there's *Gold Rush*'" He pulls up a second CD. "Or maybe we should go all the way back to *Datha*. I never play that album anymore."

I wade further into the room. "Yeah," I say. "Fab idea." I sling my thumbs in the front belt loops of my blue jeans and try to relax. "I haven't listened to that album in a dog's age." I glance about the room. "Some of those old songs still have a lot of smart stuff in them."

"*Datha* it is then." Nicki pops the CD into the stereo. "'Child on the Hill' is my favorite from this album," he says. "It's like that tune was written just for me. Like you said. Nobody really knew who that kid was. Even after they buried him." He stares at the floor for a long time. "You know, I feel like that sometimes. Buried, without a name."

My whole body is jolted by these words. I could cry. "Me too," I say, and opening up a space on the floor with the toe of my sneaker, I sit down. What a sad, sad life! How can I possibly make this boy's life a little bit brighter?

I lean back against the crossbar of the stuffed chair, hoping to relax.

"Child on the Hill" begins with the ethereal sounds of an Irish flute. My whole being feels the music. At least until Nicki clears a space beside me and sits down. I warm to his nearness and eye him through fallen shafts of hair. In a magical way, his vivid blue-green eyes, so unguarded, so otherworldly, alter the whole room, and the clutter becomes inconsequential.

Is Nicki living life the way it should be lived? Simple and direct.

No pretense. No roles. No poses.

The song's melancholic Celtic sadness carries me off to snowbound Irish churchyards and remote Scottish moors, neither of which I've ever actually experienced. But I've seen the Pinterest photos—brooding black skies, a mystical aloneness.

All of this drops down on me like a down-filled comforter.

My gaze flutters to Nicki, whose eyes are wet and swollen—or maybe I'm just imagining that. I shift my body, curling into his chest, and let his arm move across my shoulder.

"I'm so glad you're here, Chel," he says when the song ends. "I've been hoping you'd come for such a long time. I'm not nearly as lonely and alone as when I listen to that song by myself."

Look at him, you jerk, I tell myself.

"Snatch," I say, not sure anymore if I really mean that.

Things get pretty fuzzy after that. But I do remember looking at him.

"Better than Silence" is blasting from the speakers now. Overheated guitar riffs charge around the room. Dirk's drums collide with something frenzied inside me, something primal and dangerous that I've never felt before. A scream like the whine of a tuning fork stabs at my insides, stretching as taut and thin as a wire.

Nicki kisses me then, his lips soft against my teeth. I kiss him back, soulfully, so fused with the moment.

I might have stayed that way forever, safe and whole in his arms. But something has gone wrong.

Through the fog of passion, I tense as Nicki's fingers slip under my shirt. His hands, firm and calloused as parchment, stroke my bared breasts.

"Stop it." I clamp my teeth shut and press my hands against his chest. Stronger than I ever would have imagined, he pushes his body over mine and forces me onto my back.

"Don't go," he says, his voice hoarse and strained in my ear. "Everybody always goes. And I've wanted you here for so long."

I try to shift my body, but Nicki clamps an arm across my neck and rips open my shirt. He lowers his head, and when his teeth sear across one hard nipple, I beat on his back.

"Help me!" I scream, and fling my face toward the door. "Oh, God, please stop."

Nicki pulls back and smiles down on me, his small face hardened like alabaster. "It's okay, Chel," he whispers. "Honest."

"Please don't do this, Nicki." I'm terror-stricken now. My whimpers soften his face, but when he bends to kiss me again, I clamp my teeth on his lower lip. His head springs back, and splatters of blood darken the front of his crimson Datha T-shirt and dribble across my face.

"Shit." Nicki's eyes darken with pain and anger. He wipes the back of his hand across his mouth, then tears open my jeans and plunges his hand between my legs. "I thought you were different."

I scream and choke by turns.

"Can't you see?" he shouts in my face. "Can't you see that we don't ever have to be alone again? Either of us. Don't you see that?"

Tears sting my cheeks, rolling into my ears and down across my neck. I fight so hard, but Nicki only holds me tighter. Shaken and sick, pinned under him, I claw at his back. Even under these blows he forces my jeans down, opens his own, and jerks my legs apart with one bent knee.

When he enters me like a rusted knife, I fill up with acid. A searing, slamming pain beats inside me. His stinking sweat. The animal grunts. The white-hot fear and nausea. Everything in my life bruised and blackened and dead.

When he's through, he collapses beside me, limp and ragged. My body shrieks with despair. I gag again and he reaches to hold me. But I bury my face in my hands and scream again. And so he lets me go.

I don't remember how I got myself back to the dorm that night. After two a.m. the night watchman lets me in. I must be a mess. I think he asks me if I'm okay. I don't remember what I say. But the answer must satisfy him.

Stephi and Sam are both asleep. I shower, long and steamy, letting the hot water scald my skin to a pain-pale pink. In the morning, Sam asks me about my "date." I just smile weakly and tell her that I'm too busy to go into it.

PART THREE

———

The only certainty is that nothing is certain.
—PLINY THE ELDER

i

SO HERE WE ARE. MIDWEST TELECOM ARENA. CHICAGO.
September 22.

Dana has clearly exercised some clout and come up with prime front row seats for the foursome. She'd distributed these at sound check. I myself snagged a killer seat first row mid-left, thanks to Datha.com. But I managed to switch this out with a lone concertgoer for a spot right behind Annie.

A coolish evening has rolled straight out of a painfully blue Indian Summer day. Leaves crunch underfoot and an autumn nip hangs in the air, ripened with woodsmoke and moldering foliage.

As she had in April, Annie arrives first, smothered in the same enormous multicolored poncho. She has a hefty boot brace on her right foot, and she blathers on and on about summer in Scotland with Raine. Her eyes blaze with the unparalleled splendor of it all. Outside sound check, some of the younger fans took to Annie's stories like rats to poison.

Chelsea comes next, subdued and jittery, thoroughly disconnected from the rest of her Gold Rush clan. From a half dozen seats to her right, they eye her furtively, as though she could disappear. Her smiles are far too wide. Her eyes much too bright. The great gutsy glories of Annie's Celtic delusions roll off Chelsea like rain from a mallard's back.

Emily has taken up where Chelsea left off in the spring. The same backwoods Mona Lisa smile curves her thin lips, but she embodies a gorgeous optimism. Something about a challenging job and a long-overdue divorce. A new life, in short. I'm thrilled for her.

Dana shows up last, on the arm of a handsome hunk she introduces to all and sundry as one Michael Allyn—SDPD. Working security "for old time's sake." As thorny as ever, Dana dismisses Annie's Scottish fantasies, though not in so many words. In a horde of worshippers, one knotty disbeliever and a smattering of jealous malcontents can never diminish Annie's moment.

She does have a little something going for her, Annie does—Ravenhill paraphernalia of a wide variety. Pens and pins and papers. Even a small silver-plated letter opener, *RAVENHILL* etched along the handle. Raine bestowed this treasure on her in the course of her "very special" Scottish sojourn, she claims.

But a letter opener? Stationary? Not exactly the stuff of high romance. I suspect a little light-fingered pilfering myself.

Passersby stop to natter with Dana, who expounds at great length on Raine's recent marriage to Hannah Mc-Cormick, a sweet young thing from the Western Isles. Fanatics being what we are, most of us have already ingested gobs of Internet trolling on the subject. The shattering of broken hearts among the Datha faithful will rival the big bang, I expect.

Annie goes ballistic with the news and tosses off the whole affair as pure mythology. Raine would have told her, she says.

Yeah, I think. Me too. Summer has messed with Annie's head as much as it has her leg.

She's had an operation, she says, the latest in a series aimed at righting some genetic wrong. Her Velcro-ed boot brace reaches almost to her knee, and to accommodate this, her loose brown slacks have been slit halfway up the outer seam.

Raine tossed Dana another kiss when he arrived for sound check. And yes, he'd called her by name. Furthermore, Frank, a roadie we all know by sight, came out and handed her two All Access badges.

Chelsea doesn't give a hoot in hell when all these lovelies are appraised. She barely manages some mild proselytizing on a new band she's discovered—Enoch's People. I've heard of them, off and on. An English gnostic group brimming with mysticism and messianic Christianity. Up-and-coming, they are. At least they were coming up to Toronto later in the month. On the charts too, with a snappy number from their second album, *Golden Hope*, called "Devil in My Ear." Not bad for a beginner. Great percussion and a nice beat. I'd give it a seven.

Devil or not, something's burrowed into Chelsea's ear, big-time. Emily and Dana both remark on this in turn. Even I miss the bubble-headed way she had of keeping a conversation up well past its bedtime.

By way of balance to Chelsea's reserve, Emily Richards has effervesced over the summer. I find this refreshing. Chipper and flamboyant, in silky earth-mother fashion, she raves on about a full moon on a dark night. And if ever anyone stood silver in the wind like blown glass, it has to be Emily Richards.

ii

"I COULDN'T HAVE DONE ANY OF THIS WITHOUT CAITLIN. And, of course, Datha." Emily opens her smartphone and passes it to Dana. "Having them both there when I needed them was just indispensible. They showed me that I had the strength to act on the power of the words."

"Nice . . . very nice," Dana says, scrolling through the images. "So, this is part of the shop?" She taps out a cigarette and lights up.

"Oh, no . . . Hanson's is oodles bigger than that. This is *my* place." Emily beams. "It's a two-bedroom flat backed on an old Victorian at the top of Edward Street. You can just see the corner of it here. Adam Hawksworth lived there for fifty years or more. With his wife, Elizabeth. We knew each other as well as anyone. Mr. Hawksworth, bless him, passed away mid-August, and Mrs. Hawksworth took me in when I left Caitlin's. Small towns know more about you than you do yourself." Emily's eyes widen with a deep smile. "They'd kept a wild English garden out back all those years. Herbal borders, tea roses. All of it. And for free room and board, Mrs. Hawksworth has turned the whole of it over to me. It's a dream, Dana. A miraculous dream."

"Life does throw out a curve now and then, no lie," Dana says, and espying security, she grinds her smoke underfoot. "Just look at me and Michael." She downloads an abridged version of their circumstances, and then, straightening in her chair, she waves.

From a slew of red-shirted venue security personnel clumped below the stage, on the far left, Michael responds. "He thinks it's cute to moonlight on security. Says we're starting over. But we have to do it right this time. Replace all the bad memories with good ones."

Emily collects her cell phone. "I like that," she says. "Replacing old memories. And you *can* start over. If I can do this . . ."—she taps the phone's darkened screen—"anyone can."

"Maybe even your own shop one day. 'Totally savage,' as someone we know used to say." Dana's eyes flick to Chelsea, who's fidgeting to Annie's right. "Chelsea's gone off the band, I'm guessing. I've seen it before, a hundred times. All of a sudden, they don't hit the right notes anymore. And then just like that . . ."—she snaps her fingers—"it's all over and they're bored as sin."

Dana nudges Annie with her elbow. "Get a load of these garden shots of Emily's new digs, Annie. What you can't do with a little determination and a healthy dose of reality, eh?"

"Maybe you could use some of *this* stuff for *Conversations*," Annie says, whipping out a packet of her own photos. "It was really quite a trip."

"I'm sure it was." Dana makes a wry face only Emily and I can see. "The next issue's fairly cramped, what with Raine's betrothed and all."

"It isn't true, you know." Annie's face flushes. "He would have told me. What we have together is . . ."

"Very special . . . Yeah, I know," Dana says.

"No, really. He would have told me. Look at this." Annie thrusts a photo in Dana's face. "That's outside Raine's house in Duddingston, the night before I had to leave. This is Maggie Walker, his housekeeper. There's an old woman who lives right across the street. She's got the most gorgeous rose bushes. You'd love them, Emily. He always gives me a rose when I see him. I've always wondered where they come from. Well, they're this little lady's." A flat staccato chirp escapes Annie's lips. "Not this one," she says. "This is the housekeeper, Mrs. Walker. This other lady . . . across the street . . . with the roses. Raine's roses. I've pressed the last one he gave me." She opens a tour program she's retrieved from the floor. Inside I can just make out a shrunken bit of bloom the color of bad prunes. "He would have told me," Annie insists. "We're very close."

"Yeah, grew up together. I remember." Dana makes another sour face at Emily. "The rumor mill is pretty adamant about this one, Annie. I have it on pretty good authority."

"It's a lie. He wouldn't do that to me."

"To you? Chill out for God's sake, Annie."

"I'm telling you, it's not true. We were together the whole summer. Do you have any idea how hard it is for him to live like this? With all these stories? He has to find a safe place. He really needs to get away, find a safe place some-where."

Annie fumbles with the Velcro straps of her foot brace, and Dana, who's spotted Michael, says "whatever" and moves off toward him, hugging the front barrier.

Annie takes up her photo pack and swivels over to Chelsea. "This'll make you feel a lot better." She blinks in the young girl's face. "You don't look so good, Chelsea. Are you alright?"

"I'm okay. Really. I'm okay." Chelsea hauls herself to the edge of her seat and slaps her glasses back with a fist. Behind them, her eyes crawl over the crowd, left to right, right to left.

Three lanky, long-haired young men in torn blue jeans and blood-red sweat-slathered Datha T-shirts shuffle in from the far aisle to claim the empty seats to Chelsea's right. Her face hardens. The first of these men offers up a wobbly smile that makes her shudder.

"I'm just a little tired." Chelsea turns her back to the young men. "I don't sleep so good anymore."

Annie makes for her mashed rose but changes her mind. "You sure you're okay?" She sizes up the men next to Chelsea. "Those guys are real jerks. I don't know why some people even bother to come to a concert if they can't stay sober long enough to appreciate it."

"Yeah." Chelsea snatches Annie's pictures and shuffles through them with no apparent interest. "I don't think I should have come. I don't really like this new album much anymore. The whole thing doesn't do much for me. I'm working for Enoch's People now. I like their sound. It's clear, straightforward." Chelsea tilts forward over Annie's chair. "I know this is stupid," she says. "But can I trade places with you? These guys are freaking me out."

"Sure . . . no problem." Annie gathers up her poncho, her photos, her program, her dead rose, and slides into Chelsea's seat, Chelsea into hers.

Dana returns, and Annie fetches up her rose for renewed consideration.

But it's too late. The house lights drop, the stage goes black, and the opening chords of "Speaking Eyes" slide over a tumultuous roar.

Emily

I'M AWASH IN THE BAND'S SPIRIT AND ENERGY. APRIL'S show had been only a fleeting escape. The same lurid terrors sprang up when all the songs were sung, and reality beat me down again with both fists.

All those shadows are gone now. Shane will be a force in my life until child support issues are resolved. But the papers have been served, the decree has been issued, and though sometimes, in the dread of night, the old horrors rear up, I'm free.

By the grace of God, Shane's company transferred him to Dayton, effective at the end of the month. All the pleading phone calls, all the desperate regret, will end then. Shane's never been one to spend a dime where a penny will do.

This liberation, I know, can only be placed on my own slim shoulders. Yet without Caitlin and without Datha, I may never have gathered sufficient courage. Caitlin I have already blessed in person. But how to repay these talented young men onstage, unknown and unknowable? I can only revel in their moment, commend them from my heart, for having carried me into a new beginning.

Annie

(In Her Own Words)

RAINE HOLDS ME SPELLBOUND, SHOWS ME HIS APPROVAL, his affection, his love. All the things we share. He'll always be mine. Nothing matters beyond him. Nothing matters without him. All these dippy Datha banners draped all over like dirty laundry. Flags waving. Clumps of flowers. Batches of balloons. He's surrounded by stupidity and lust. All he has to give wrapped up in *Let it Raine* on somebody's sweaty T-shirt. It all makes me quite sick.

Far, far away, there must be a place where he can be safe. For his sake, I'll find that place. Isn't death . . . that sweet escape I've planned for him for weeks now . . . isn't death the best gift I can give him?

And yet . . . he's so . . . *special*, so separate from all the wheedling hangers-on. At least on stage. This wedding thing, this Hannah from the Western Isles, none of that can be true. I can see that now, in the way he looks at me.

By Datha's third number, "My Father's Scottish Son," which slides—as always—into "Perfect Corruption," I've reconsidered.

I'd been fully prepared to be outed by venue metal detectors. Raine's release was worth any risk. But with my crutches—stretched out now against the front barricade—security slacked off when I limped through the entrance queue. No search. No pat down. No hand wand. Only a raft of "so sorry's," some sympathetic teasing, and a shuffling bypass of the awkward detector. The weight of Leon's Smith and Wesson—taped to my leg under the boot—has only added to the growing throb in my leg.

The crowd is bonkers now.

How deeply loved he is. How much more he still has to give.

Not yet, I tell myself. Death is not yet the answer. And prying the gun free, with a sharp kick I chuck it under my chair.

Dana

(In Her Own Words)

A DAMN FINE-LOOKING MAN. SWEET AND GENTLE. THE sexy body, all that gorgeous sloe-black hair. The music will always be extraordinary. The friendship intact and un-matched. But Raine is no longer that unreachable tickle in my heart, the one man I want alone in a dark room. In fact, I don't want him at all. I love Michael—more than life itself. And there's an unspeakable joy in that.

Raine's wedding has come and gone. We'll welcome his bride, Hannah McCormick, later tonight, at a backstage post-concert reception. Happiness, friendship, and enduring goodwill are all I have left to give him.

Michael and I have worked hand in hand to structure the substance abuse program for the district's fall semester. I still marvel at how completely he understands me and supports my psyche, both personally and professionally—my strengths, my weaknesses, my convictions.

With the launch of "Better than Silence," the concert draws to a close. My eyes drift to Michael as he makes his way to me though the rank and file of gathered venue secu-rity. Even in the darkness, his long body moves as sure, as smooth, as confident as a panther's.

Oh, to roll myself in _that_ man's arms again.

Chelsea

(In Her Own Words)

TWO TORTURED HOURS. ALL I CAN THINK OF IS GETTING out and away.

I lean toward Annie. But she sidesteps, and those awful men loom larger. My head buzzes, my skin prickles with a rising heat, and sharp rasps like the panting of a hunted animal escape my lips.

No more encores. Please. No more encores.

My eyes blink into the crowd. "I have to go," I say. But the music roars on.

Too many people. Too much noise. The pressing, pushing, shoving, poking, prodding.

Why did I come? How can I stay?

I clap my hands over my ears. "Please let me out," I say to Annie, but of course, with the roar of "Better than Silence," she can't possibly hear me. Nausea springs up at the back of my throat.

I strain to settle myself in the safety of my dorm room— the pale lace curtains at the window, the hum of the ceiling fan, a summer breeze whispering across the oak-wood floors.

"You're alright," I whisper. I take a deep breath, and the terror subsides.

But then I open my eyes again, and he's there! Nicki! In his blood-red Datha T-shirt. He's coming to hurt me again.

Is he talking to me?

He's talking to me!

"No, please don't."

A shock of white blinds my eyes as the house lights come up. The crowd melds to a wriggling mass of color and sound.

Choking on my own sobs, I drop to the floor, groping under the seat on my hands and knees, desperate for any escape.

Oh, God! He's found me! He's here, right above me!

I jump to my feet, a revolver clasped between my hands.

One sharp crack and I snap back into the conscious present. Beside me, a woman's familiar face swells with horror.

"Michael!" she shrieks.

PART FOUR

———

In the end there is only light and dark.
And the two are not so far apart.
—THOMAS LLOYD QUALLS

MICHAEL ALLYN LIES CRUMPLED ON THE FLOOR. THE front of his red *MTA Security* shirt is soaked in blood like spilled wine. His head and shoulders rest in Dana's lap. She's staring from her right hand, sticky with blood, to his face, now the color of cold ashes. And all the time, she's been begging for help.

Within minutes, paramedics hoist Michael's limp body onto a metal stretcher and haul him away, Dana in tow. The authorities follow with Chelsea.

The media, online and off, pitches the incident as it happens, trending with #DathaConcertShooting, #SDPD-CopShot, #MTAChicago, #MidwestTelecomLockdown, and variations along the lines of: *Distraught Datha Fan Fires on Security at Chicago Concert.* And with that, a blizzard of tropes of Chelsea Davis in custody. By all accounts, she flipped out, having been brutally attacked over the summer by some red-shirted Gold Rush creep.

No one knows much about the gun—a Smith and Wesson 642 Airweight. No markings, no serial number. It's not Chelsea's, that much is clear. They'll trace the thing, everyone says. It's only a matter of time.

SHOT IN THE CHEST AT POINT-BLANK RANGE, IT'S TOUCH and go for Michael for three days. A working cop on some nostalgia binge and he's slammed like gang scum.

Just before Halloween, I Skype-message Dana about a concert review I've been working on for *Conversations.* Michael has fully recovered, she says. Proposed the day he regained consciousness from the six-hour operation that removed bullet fragments from near his spine. They're to be married early next year.

I rejoice. I'm a sucker for happy endings.

Chelsea Davis, arraigned on assault charges, is remanded

to the custody of her parents, a pair of well-heeled Toronto highbrows. They'll see to it that she does long-term quality time with some big-name shrink. The low-life vermin who jumped her—Nicki somebody—is nowhere to be found, but heads are set to roll mightily at the MTA.

Do I remember a couple of Scottish digital photos posted to *Conversations*' website last month, Dana asks? Duddingston. Ravenhill. Edinburgh.

And of course, I do.

Annie Brenner's, she says. And, well . . . Emily Richards—who's blogging for *Conversations* at this point—sent her a text to say Annie had been arrested in Chicago earlier in the week on charges of theft, news that just popped up on Instagram and my Facebook feed. No surprise there, I guess.

But get this—involuntary manslaughter is in the mix.

Seems some Q-tip in Annie's orbit died suddenly. Something about filched funds and altered medication. And . . . the gun Chelsea used had been ripped off from a South Side Chicago pawnshop—by Annie Brenner.

Any way you slice it, Annie's in deep shit.

I can't say I expected that foursome to fit the frame as well as they did. But then I'm not exactly tripped out about it either.

We hard-core fans can be a scary lot. Some of us will do just about anything.

ACKNOWLEDGMENTS

"Ella (An Artificial Lotus Blossom)" was long-listed with the Frome Short Story Competition.

"Melody Rose (An Empty Ketchup Holder)" was long-listed with the Fish International Prize.

"Robin (The Handle of a Child's Bucket)" was a finalist with the Tucson Book Festival, short-listed and previously published by Retreat West in 2017.

"Verna (A Jar of Pickled Onions)" was a finalist with *The Pinch.*

"Scilla (A Wine Bottle Cork)" was previously published with Momaya Press in 2016.

"Brook (A Packet of Arthritis Pills)" was previously published with the *Potomac Review* in 2018 and won Honorable Mention for Published Short Stories/Single Story with the 2019 National Federation of Press Women's Communications Contest.

ABOUT THE AUTHOR

CREDIT: DESIGN PHOTOGRAPHY

DIANNE EBERTT BEEAFF is the award-winning author of five previous books. She has been a freelance writer for many years, beginning in the area of magazine journalism. She is a member of the Women's Fiction Writers Association, Arizona Professional Writers, The National Federation of Press Women, The Authors Guild, PEN America, and the Society of Southwestern Authors. As an artist, Dianne works primarily in graphite and watercolor, and her work has been shown in a variety of local, national, and international galleries. She lives in Tucson, Arizona, with her husband, Dan.

Dianne's work may be seen at
www.debeeaff.wordpress.com

Our Love Could Light the World by Anne Leigh Parrish. $15.95,
978-1-938314-44-5. Twelve stories depicting a dysfunctional and
chaotic—yet lovable—family that has to band together in order to
survive.

True Stories at the Smoky View by Jill McCroskey Coupe. $16.95,
978-1-63152-051-8. The lives of a librarian and a ten-year-old boy are
changed forever when they become stranded by a blizzard in a
Tennessee motel and join forces in a very personal search for justice.

The Moon Always Rising by Alice C. Early. $16.95,
978-1-63152-683-1. When Eleanor "Els" Gordon's life cracks apart,
she exiles herself to a derelict plantation house on the Caribbean
island of Nevis—and discovers, with the help of her resident ghost,
that only through love and forgiveness can she untangle years-old
family secrets and set herself free to love again.

The End of Miracles by Monica Starkman. $16.95, 978-1-63152-054-9.
When a pregnancy following years of infertility ends in late
miscarriage, Margo Kerber sinks into a depression—one that leads her,
when she encounters a briefly unattended baby, to commit an
unthinkable crime.

Profound and Perfect Things by Maribel Garcia. $16.95,
978-1631525414. When Isa, a closeted lesbian with conservative
Mexican parents, has a one-night stand that results in an unwanted
pregnancy, her sister, Cristina adopts the baby—but twelve years
later, Isa, who regrets giving up her child, threatens to spill the secret
of her daughter's true parentage.

A Drop in the Ocean: A Novel by Jenni Ogden. $16.95,
978-1-63152-026-6. When middle-aged Anna Fergusson's research lab
is abruptly closed, she flees Boston to an island on Australia's Great
Barrier Reef—where, amongst the seabirds, nesting turtles, and
eccentric islanders, she finds a family and learns some bittersweet
lessons about love.